A Wir

ROBIN MERRILL

New Creation Publishing
Madison, Maine

Chapter 1

"**O**w!" Joanna gave her own neck a mighty slap, but it was too late.

Sandra knew by the sound of Joanna's cry that it had been a deer fly, which, for some reason, the locals insisted on calling copperheads. The first several times a Mainer had told her they'd been bitten by a copperhead, she'd wondered when snakes had learned to fly. But now she knew the lingo. Most of it, most of the time.

"Can I have more oil?" Joanna asked, meaning citronella oil, which kept the mosquitoes at bay.

"Sorry, honey. That won't do anything for the copperheads." A bat cracked, and Sandra tried to be gentle as she nudged her daughter aside so she could see one of their church elders sprinting toward first base. Most people wouldn't have known that he was sprinting, but Sandra had seen him jog before. The spry young man playing shortstop for Grace Evangelical easily threw poor Elder Mashman out, who, appearing to take the whole thing personally, turned and trudged back toward their dugout. Sandra, the reluctant scorekeeper, was relieved that most of the team hung out *behind* the dugout; otherwise, it would be mighty crowded on her bench. She wrote the out in the scorebook and then tried to focus on the next at bat, though Joanna was now chattering away about some pony she'd seen on YouTube. Sandra nodded absentmindedly, watched the batter strike out, noted it in the book, and then looked around for her husband, the one who'd talked her into this grand service opportunity and was now off yukking it up with the people in the bleachers.

She couldn't believe a church game could have so many spectators, but there they were. This was the Provost family's first year of church softball. Nate had played years ago, but this was his first year with her in tow, and she wasn't yet sure how she felt about it. Oh sure, it was good to get outside and hang out with people from church, getting some exercise. It was also a giant pain in the butt to do it with three kids. Eleven-year-old Peter, her oldest, wanted to play, but those in charge said he was too young, and now he was sulking in the minivan, staring down at his iPad. So much for *his* fresh air and exercise.

Finally, the umpire called the third out, and Sandra said a silent prayer of gratitude. It was true that she was supposed to be cheering for her team to *not* get any outs, but she just wanted to go home. There was a well-worn couch and some leftover tuna noodle casserole calling her name.

The New Hope Church coed softball team trotted out onto the field and took their positions. League rules allowed for ten players on the field, and that's exactly how many players had shown up tonight. Grace Evangelical, known more often as simply Grace E, so that it sounded like people were cheering for a little girl named Gracie whenever they hollered their support, had a deeper bench that seemed to be full of ringers. Or maybe New Hope was just that terrible. This was their third game of the season, and they'd yet to get one in the win column, but Sandra certainly couldn't be bothered to care. Her husband seemed to be enjoying himself, and they were doing something as a family—sort of. So she tried to enjoy it.

Grace E's runs came in so fast that her pencil had trouble keeping up. Every time she looked down to record something, the runners would advance another base or two, and these people weren't wearing numbers on their backs, so they were impossible to keep track of. She'd written little notes to herself along Grace E's lineup. Next to "Bill," she'd written "red hat." Next to "Mike," she'd written "loud wife." Still, it was hard to keep up, and when the lead crept past ten runs, she stopped worrying about accuracy. No one was ever going to look at this scorebook, anyway.

The New Hope team was so bad that they made her catcher-husband Nate look like an all-star. He was helped out by a truly talented first baseman who went by the name of Boomer. She'd only recently learned why—he could hit the ball impressively far. But after that, the pickings were slim. Everyone insisted this was okay, of course, that they were just out there to have fun. Yet, they cheered their heads off when Nate finally threw the ball to first for the third out. So maybe they didn't like losing as much as they let on. Or maybe they just were really excited to bat.

Several of them tossed their gloves into the dugout, one of them hitting Sammy squarely in the back of the stroller. He didn't seem to mind. He just stared up at the sky, making her wonder if their church angel was in charge of overseeing softball games, or if that fell under someone else's jurisdiction.

"Lineup!" Lewis snapped as if he'd already asked for the lineup ten times. Maybe he had. She had no idea. But she could understand why no one remembered who was up. Their last at bat had happened hours ago. She flipped the book over and read off the names of the next three batters. Lewis didn't thank her. She wasn't surprised.

Grace E put in a different pitcher, who was a smidge slower than the first. She wondered what it would be like to be on a team that had more than one pitcher. "Go Grac-*eeee*!" The high-pitched peal came from the bleachers along the first base line. Mike's wife.

Pastor Cliff, looking official, sauntered into the third base coaching box. Sandra tried not to roll her eyes. She loved her pastor. She really did. He was a wonderful pastor. But he took this whole softball thing, and his role as leader of it, a little too seriously.

New Hope's first batter stepped up to the plate and hit a grounder directly to the first baseman. One out. Sandra's tuna noodle casserole fantasy grew more intense. Their second batter stepped up and hit the world's teeniest pop fly to the pitcher. *At least they're hitting the ball. Sort of.* The third batter, Steve York, shuffled into the batters' box, looking so uncomfortable that Sandra wondered if he had itching powder in his pants. The first pitch was met with the world's most awkward swing, and a *ping* sound sent the ball up the middle. Everyone was surprised, especially Steve, who took a few seconds to process the idea that he was now supposed to run. Mild-mannered Pastor Cliff was screaming at him to go, and finally, Steve went. He took off like a dump truck shifting through gears and by the time he reached first, he was traveling at a pretty good clip, with significant momentum. That's what made it quite so tragic when his foot hit the bag at an odd angle and sent him spilling into the grass and rolling toward the fence—howling.

Chapter 2

The field fell silent. "Safe!" the umpire interrupted the silence and then called a timeout. No one rushed to Steve's aid, and Sandra scanned the bleachers and parking lot for Steve's wife, but she wasn't there. *Smart woman*, Sandra thought. Joanna gave her a questioning look, and Sandra wondered if she'd said the thought aloud.

After more than a minute of Steve writhing around on the ground in agony, a woman climbed out of the bleachers. Sandra knew her by sight, but not by name. Their church was just big enough that, if one didn't sit on the same side as someone, and didn't participate in the same activities or ministries, one might never learn that person's name. Whatever her name was, Sandra overheard her tell the umpire that she was a paramedic and ask permission before going out onto the field. She probably didn't need permission, as by this time, Steve had rolled mostly off the field, but he might still have technically been in play.

With permission granted, the kind Samaritan trotted to Steve's side. They had a brief, intimate conversation, and then she helped him to his feet. This brought applause from both sets of bleachers. He could hardly walk and placed all his weight on his new friend's slim shoulder.

"We need a base runner!" Pastor Cliff hollered toward the dugout.

Just whom was he talking to? They didn't have any extra players. She tried to convey this message to him with a facial expression, but his eyes didn't rest on her long enough to receive any message.

He looked at the umpire. "We need a base runner!" he cried, as if this was the umpire's problem to solve.

The umpire clearly didn't care. He shrugged. "You need a sub."

Again, Pastor looked into the almost empty dugout. Good thing Peter was in the minivan, or he would've been drafted. And though he likely would've been pleased at the development, Sandra didn't want him drafted to run bases one time only to get booted again. That would have been too emotionally jarring, so she didn't volunteer him.

Neither did her husband. Instead, Nate looked at her, his eyes wide.

She shook her head slowly and dramatically, telling him with her eyes that she would rather die than be a pinch runner in flip flops.

Nate quickly dropped this idea—he'd always been a wise man—and looked into the New Hope bleachers. Suddenly, he pointed at someone. "You're wearing sneakers! Would you come run for us?"

Sandra snickered at the long list of qualifications. She squinted into the crowd to try to figure out whom Nate was addressing, but she couldn't tell. Then a slim young man wearing too many clothes for June looked over each of his shoulders and then looked at Nate. "Me?" Nate had picked out the only male over the age of twelve—a fairly sexist selection for a co-ed team. But, taking a quick census of who else was in the bleachers, Sandra couldn't imagine any of the women doing it. Any woman who wanted to play was already in the game. Both of them.

"Yes!" Nate appeared to be genuinely excited. "What's your name?"

The young recruit's demeanor did not match Nate's enthusiasm. "Phoenix." He slowly rose to his feet and began a gradual descent out of the bleachers.

"Well, Phoenix, nice to meet you. Would you do us a solid and come run around the bases once?"

It was clear that Phoenix did not want to do this. He stood there as if waiting for someone to intervene and save him.

No one did.

Gingerly, he peeled off his scuffed leather jacket and dropped it into the grass. Then he unbuttoned his flannel shirt with painful slowness before it joined its leather companion on the ground. Sandra admired the umpire's patience. She knew he wasn't getting paid by the hour. Phoenix's undressing revealed an electric blue T-shirt that read "Hope House" over a drawing of a building. He ran a nervous hand through his greasy hair and then strode toward the unoccupied first base.

"Wait, wait, wait!" someone called from the other dugout. He headed out toward the umpire, whom Sandra didn't envy right now. In fact, she felt her body bristling against whatever was about to be thrown at him. "They can't just pull someone off the bleachers! He's not on the roster!"

The umpire appeared to have no idea whether this was true. Neither did he appear to care one way or the other.

"Yes, we can!" Nate raised his hand as if waiting for the umpire to call on him to speak, except that he didn't wait. He dropped his hand and walked toward home plate. "It's right in our league rules, sir. We can add someone to the roster at any point in the game."

This made sense. This was *church* softball, after all, which was, as far as she knew, supposed to be a ministry. Didn't want to be turning people away just because they showed up late to a game. Or because they showed up with absolutely no intention of participating.

The Grace E coach stood there staring at Nate and shuffling his feet and then must have decided to surrender, because he wordlessly turned and headed back to the dugout.

Sandra glanced at the silent bleachers. Everyone was staring at the new guy on first base. Even the kids. Sandra scanned the faces of the spectators and then of the team to see if anyone seemed to know Phoenix, but they all looked baffled. Phoenix pulled up his baggy black jeans, but they immediately fell back down. The multiple pockets seemed to be full of lead balls, and the back of his frayed hems rested in the dirt.

No one made any attempt to add him to any roster or official scorecard. Sandra could hardly blame the ump for not bothering. Perhaps he had his own tuna noodle casserole to get home to.

Chapter 3

G race E threw Phoenix out at second base, making the whole endeavor to find and employ a pinch runner seem like a big waste of time.

But as Phoenix strode off the field, Nate ran out to greet him and pumped his hand up and down. Sandra expected poor Phoenix to return to the bleachers from whence he came, but from somewhere Nate produced an old, floppy glove and sent him to short field. Sandra couldn't tell whether Phoenix *wanted* this to happen, but he didn't look upset by the development. In fact, she couldn't read him at all. He just stood there staring at the back of the shortstop's head.

Perhaps Phoenix knew, after watching only a few innings, how absurd it was that Richard Barney was playing shortstop. He was a slow, giant man. But Richard Barney *wanted* to play shortstop, and so he did. Because no one in their church said no to the Barneys. About anything.

Grace E batted the ball all over the field, and while it never went near the enigmatic Phoenix, he never moved his feet either. Again and again the ball scooted past Richard and rolled within fielding distance of Phoenix, but he was content to let the left fielder or the center fielder do the duties. Sandra could hardly blame him. And even when the center fielder did pick the ball up and attempt to throw it into the infield, Phoenix didn't even watch this happen. He just stood there staring straight ahead.

The only time Sandra saw him move happened in the fifth inning. He did not back up a throw to third—of course he didn't—and third baseman Brendan Barney, son of the great Richard, embarrassed that he'd missed the play, hollered at Phoenix for not having his back. At this, Phoenix's head did swivel in Brendan's direction, his eyes giving him a sizzling look that could've melted glass. Apparently, Phoenix didn't like being hollered at by a short man with a big ego. Not for the first time, Sandra wondered how Brendan could so *not* resemble his father, who almost doubled his height.

Sandra wouldn't admit it to anyone, but she couldn't stand Brendan Barney. In fact, she secretly blamed him for their softball team's dwindling numbers. They'd had more than enough players that first night, but each time Brendan hollered at someone, the lucky recipient didn't bother to come back. Nate told her she was crazy, that people had thicker skin than that, and that people were just busy this time of year, but she wasn't so sure. She thought Brendan made their whole church family look bad. She sneaked a glance at Brendan's wife, but she was so busy with her small tribe of children that she appeared unaware that her husband was verbally abusing someone again. Sandra fervently hoped that Brendan didn't talk to his wife like that. Or his multitudinous children.

Having completely abandoned her task of keeping score—they were going to get mercied, after all—Sandra tried to count Daphne Barney's children, but they wouldn't hold still. There were at least four of them, maybe as many as six. Or seven? All girls. And their names all started with B, something Sandra thought was probably Brendan's doing, not Daphne's. Sandra knew the oldest, Bethany, because she was Peter's age. The rest of them all sort of melded into one busy B-shaped blur. Poor Daphne.

At long last, the game ended, and Sandra had to force Joanna to stop carving her masterpiece into the dirt floor of the dugout with a stick. Joanna wasn't happy about this, but Sandra didn't care. Sammy was asleep in his stroller, and Sandra was jealous. She handed the scorebook off to Pastor Cliff and then, pushing Sammy with one hand and pulling Joanna with the other, headed toward the refuge of her minivan.

The siren didn't sound until the cruiser was directly behind her, so when it did chirp, it scared the tar out of her. Sammy's eyes popped open and he didn't even hesitate; his little mouth opened and the volume of his wail rivaled that of the cop car. Sandra turned to look at the car and then squinted; though it wasn't dark out yet, the flashing blue lights were still blinding. Why was a cop car sneaking up on her and then turning on its lights and siren? Two uniformed officers jumped out of the car and started running for the woods. What on earth? She turned to look in the direction they were headed and saw her favorite pinch runner approaching the forest. *Oh wow!* Her pulse quickened.

"Mama? Who are the police chasing?"

She didn't answer Joanna. She was too busy watching, as was everyone else in the parking lot. Phoenix disappeared into the trees and then, ten seconds later, so did the policemen. She still stood there watching, though. She didn't want to miss anything. They had to come out of the woods eventually.

Nate appeared beside her and put his hand on her back. "Come on, Sandy, let's get the kids home."

She ripped her eyes away from the woods to look at her husband. "What was that all about?"

"No idea. I guess our pinch runner is about to get pinched." He laughed at his own joke, and then took the stroller from her and pushed it toward their van. Joanna followed her dad. Sandra stood rooted to her spot, the tuna noodle casserole forgotten. Where did Phoenix think he was going? There was nothing on the other side of that woods, not for miles. And how had the police known that he was there? Had they been following him and had just finally caught up, or had someone called them? She looked around at the rapidly dissipating crowd. Did someone here know who Phoenix was and that he was wanted by the police? If they did, they weren't letting on.

Her minivan rolled to a stop beside her. "Get in, Sandy." Nate was irritated, so she acquiesced, even though her feet felt like lead blocks. They didn't want to go anywhere.

Chapter 4

When Nate pulled his family's minivan into the large church parking lot on Sunday morning, Sandra gasped. Parked in the corner of the lot, near the outfield fence of the softball field, were three police cars. A gaggle of people, some in blue uniforms and some not, stood at the edge of the woods.

"What's going on?" Peter asked from the back.

"No," Nate said.

"No what?" Sandra was unsure what or whom Nate was saying no to.

"Just no. We are going to walk into church, and you are not going to get involved."

Sandra made a derisive *pff* sound. "Get involved? What are you talking about? We don't even know what happened!"

"Exactly, and yet I can feel you already thinking about calling Bob."

He was exaggerating. She hadn't been thinking that. Police activity didn't automatically warrant a call to the local middle school sports angel. She would at least find out if there was any reason to call him first. She caught herself hoping there *was* a reason to call him and then mentally slapped herself. Yes, she missed her angel friend, but she didn't need to go wishing for tragedy so that she had an excuse to hang out with him.

Nate pulled the van into the parking spot furthest away from the action.

Like this was going to stop her.

"Dad, why did you park so far?" Joanna asked. The kid had a point.

"Dad's afraid Mom is going to go all super sleuth again," Peter explained, and though he said it without an ounce of respect, Sandra took it as a compliment and tried not to let her proud smile beam too brightly.

"There may be nothing to sleuth about." Sandra tried to sound demure. She failed.

"Oh sure," Nate said, "I'm sure that *three* state trooper cars means someone lost a kitten." He blew out a puff of air that made his bangs twitch. "I just hope no one's been killed this time."

Sandra had a feeling this wasn't going to be the case. The image of Phoenix running into those same woods on Tuesday night flashed through her mind and she shivered.

"What?" Nate asked. He was observing her far more closely than he usually did.

"Nothing. Just got a chill." This made no sense. It was already seventy-five degrees outside, and Nate still had the van's heater blowing on her toes.

Peter read her mind. "Do you think it has something to do with that guy who played in the softball game?"

"Don't know," Sandra said. But she was pretty sure that it did. There just wasn't that much action in her small town. What were the chances of two dramas unfolding in the same patch of Plainfield forest?

"Did they ever catch that guy?" Peter asked.

Sandra opened her mouth to answer him, but Nate beat her to it. "Though your mother has been glued to all news media for the last four days, she hasn't heard a peep, so we don't know. But I can tell you that he's not that dangerous of a criminal, or it would have been on the news whether they caught him or not."

"Can we go in?" Joanna asked. "I'm scared."

"Of course, honey, and there's nothing to be scared of. The police are here. I'm sure they have everything under control." Trying not to stare at the edge of the forest, Sandra slid out of the van and then opened the sliding door to spring her youngest from his car seat. She grabbed the diaper bag and turned to head for the church—again, trying not to stare at the woods.

Nate scooted ahead of her and opened the church door for her and then she was inside, where the quiet calm hit her like a sopping wet blanket. *Now* what was she going to do? All the action was outside, and now she couldn't even sneak a peek! She swallowed hard and told herself it was none of her business. *I'm not really a sleuth. I've just gotten into a few odd situations. Doesn't mean I'll ever get into another one. Right? Maybe.* True, she didn't want to get trapped or assaulted ever again, and she didn't want to fear for her life ever again, but whatever puzzle was currently laid out at the corner of the woods—well, she *really* wanted to help put it together.

"It's not my place," she muttered aloud as she entered the room full of well-worn rocking chairs. It was her turn for Sunday school nursery duty, so she couldn't exactly sneak away to spy on the cops, at least, not without a trail of babies in walkers following her across the parking lot. She could envision it and shuddered at the thought. She flicked on the lights and looked around the cluttered room. No, she would *not* go find out why the police were in the woods behind the church. She would stay in the nursery, right where she was supposed to be.

She even avoided the urge to ask every mom who came in to drop off a baby if they knew anything. Most of these mothers asked *her* if she knew anything. But no one knew anything—until Ethel came in.

"How do *you* know what's going on?" Sandra asked her kids' beloved babysitter.

Ethel raised her eyebrows and tilted her head to the side. "Because I went and asked them. Why, I watched Chip Buker grow up in this very church! In fact, I used to wipe his hiney right in this very nursery! He'd better tell me what's what!"

"Well?" Sandra pushed. "What *is* what?"

Ethel leaned in closer but didn't lower her voice. "He wouldn't tell me who, but there's a body in the woods."

Sandra's stomach sank. She'd wanted a puzzle to solve, yes, but she hadn't wanted another death. "He told you that?"

Ethel looked at the carpet. "No, but there's a van marked coroner here." They stood there together for a silent moment. Then Ethel said, "Why don't you go see what you can find out? I'll stay behind with the babies."

Sandra had never left a nursery so fast.

Chapter 5

Sandra crossed the parking lot toward the activity on the edge of the woods. She tried to act naturally, as if she had every reason in the world to approach a crime scene. Of course, she didn't know for sure yet that it was a crime scene, but it looked that way. The entire trip across the lot, she had to fight the urge to look back over her shoulder to make sure she wasn't actually being followed by an entourage of toddlers pushing corn popper toys.

She'd just stepped off the asphalt and onto the freshly mowed lawn, about fifty yards from the action, when a man in uniform stopped her. She wondered, not for the first time, why Maine state troopers wore such giant hats. "I'm sorry, ma'am. Necessary personnel only."

She tried to smile at him, but she knew it probably looked creepy. She'd never been good at fake smiling. Her mind raced to think of something to say. Why hadn't she prepared questions in advance? She was nowhere near the super sleuth her son thought she was. "Is someone hurt?" she managed. *Pathetic.*

"I'm sorry. I can't say." He glanced over her head. "Do you go to church here?"

As she nodded, she saw Detective Chip Buker in the distance.

"You should go back inside," the phlegmatic officer said.

"Chip!" she called out. "Chip! Over here!" The embarrassment was almost overwhelming. The trooper looked amused and turned to look in Chip's direction. She opened her mouth to shout his name again but then didn't, because he glanced her way. She gave him an overly enthusiastic wave instead, feeling a little like a fan girl leaning on the

16

ropes at a sold-out Garth Brooks concert. Much to her amazement, Chip headed her way. Wonders never ceased.

"Hi, Sandra." He glanced at his subordinate and then back to her. "What can I do for you?"

"Hi, Detective Buker." She tried to sound appropriately respectful. "Who died?"

He stared at her as if he couldn't decide whether to answer her, and though she returned his gaze, her peripheral vision caught Detective Slaughter looking at them suspiciously from a couple hundred feet away. *Please do not come over here.* Slaughter was such a party pooper.

"You go to church here?" Chip asked.

Why was that such a popular question? "Yes, why?" But as soon as she asked why, she realized that if she *didn't* go to church there, it would be way weirder that she'd shown up at their crime scene. In pumps.

He didn't answer her question. He still appeared to be attempting to solve some complex puzzle in his head. She forced herself to be quiet and patient as he did so. Finally, he nodded and said, "Come with me."

She hadn't completed her first step before Slaughter stomped their way. She wore a black pantsuit that seemed out of place on a Sunday morning in western Maine. It also looked very warm. How was she not sweating to death? She met them halfway across the lawn, trying to murder Chip with her eyes. "What are you doing?"

Chip stopped walking, so Sandra stopped too, even though an invisible force was pulling her toward the forest. "I'm going to ask her if she recognizes the victim. She goes to church here."

Sandra blinked. Did Chip not know who the victim was? If not, then it probably wasn't Phoenix, because the cops obviously knew who he was.

Slaughter narrowed her eyes so efficiently they were almost shut. "Dozens of other people go to this church too. Let's pick one of them"—her eyes threw some disdain Sandra's way—"not someone who thinks she's Miss Marple."

Sandra couldn't be sure, but she thought she saw defensiveness in Chip's eyes. She couldn't imagine why he'd be defensive of her. Detective Slaughter wasn't entirely off base.

"Karen, relax. She's not after your job, and"—he looked at Sandra—"though I can't explain it, she seems to have an aptitude for this." He returned his gaze to Slaughter. "Let's just see if she knows him. And either way, she can keep her eyes and ears open and then"—his tone turned stern— "she will report back to us." He gave her a closed-lipped smile. "Right, Ms. Provost?"

"Right," Sandra said without thinking about it.

"Good. Because Detective Slaughter is correct in saying that *you* are not a detective."

"Right," she said again, bouncing on her heels in impatience.

"Right. And we don't want you putting yourself in danger again. So, you'll call us the second you hear, see, or think of anything."

"Right." It was much easier to be patient with children.

"Okay then. This way." He started walking.

Disagreement and disdain rolled off Slaughter in waves, stinging Sandra's skin as she picked up her pace to get away from her. But Slaughter fell into step behind them, leaving Sandra with the uneasy sensation that at any second she was about to be stabbed in the kidney. She couldn't even blame the woman. If Sandra was objective about it, she'd probably even side with her. Why on earth was Chip being so forthcoming? It was true that Franklin County had only suffered two murders in the last year, and she *had* pretty much solved both of them, but that had been mostly thanks to heavenly help. Of course, Chip didn't know that. So maybe he did think she had some super-sleuth-skill. She bit back a smirk. She liked the idea that he might think such a thing.

She stepped into the shade of the trees and the temperature immediately dropped. Black flies appeared out of nowhere and buzzed around her face. She tried to wave them off with one hand, but it was like trying to wave away air. More air just flooded in. She squinted to keep them out of her eyes and followed Chip toward the commotion, which she soon saw to be about a dozen people forming a perimeter around a man lying on the ground. Her skin grew cold. She didn't need to see his face to know who it was. He wore the same leather jacket and the same baggy black jeans. A man in uniform crouched nearby photographing the body, which lay on its side, almost in the fetal position, but with one arm flung out to the side as if reaching for something. The idea of his reaching through the ferns for help sent a shudder through her body. Maybe she *shouldn't* have pushed her way into this situation. Suddenly, the nursery didn't seem so bad.

Chapter 6

"His name is Phoenix." Sandra's voice cracked on his name and she envied Slaughter's stoicism. Though Phoenix had never seemed animated to begin with, Sandra found his current stillness deeply disturbing. She looked at Chip. "At least, that's what he said his name was. Does he have a driver's license on him?"

"Huh. We didn't think to look for that," Slaughter snarled.

"No wallet. Did Phoenix give you a last name?"

Sandra stared at Chip. "How do you not know who this is? I watched police chase him into these same woods on Tuesday."

"What?" Slaughter cried. Not so stoical all of a sudden.

Sandra looked at Slaughter's open mouth, then at Chip, and then back to Slaughter. They appeared to be telepathically communicating. Slaughter's surprise morphed into anger. Chip just looked embarrassed. Finally, Slaughter looked at her. "Was it the Sheriff's Department?"

Sandra shook her head. "Town police."

Slaughter put her hands on her hips. "Of course. Those imbeciles."

Chip stepped closer to Sandra. "Would you do me a huge favor?"

She didn't need him to elaborate. She was embarrassed for them. "I won't tell a soul."

"Thank you." He took his phone out of his pocket and scrolled through a list of numbers before hitting the call button. Sandra held her breath as he talked to someone at Plainfield PD. She was impressed by his ability to get the information he needed without letting on that the State Police had been completely clueless as to Phoenix's identity two minutes ago.

"I take it they don't know much?" Slaughter asked after he hung up. She dragged the toe of her black Dansko through the soft earth, like a bull pawing at the ground before charging. Sandra shuffled away from her and closer to Chip.

He slid his phone back into his pocket. "No, but his name is indeed Phoenix, and we even have a last name now. Haynes. He's got a record, but he's managed to stay out of trouble for the last several years. Someone called them and said Bill Jackson was on the property. Then when they got here, this guy took off running, so they pursued. But obviously, he's not Bill Jackson." He stared down at Phoenix's motionless body.

"Who's Bill Jackson?"

Slaughter curled a lip. "Bad news, that's who. So, someone just called in a false tip? How helpful. Bet they'd like to know who that was."

Chip nodded, his jaw tight.

"Are they going to trace the number?"

"Already did. Burner."

Sandra made a mental note that they were called burners, not fire phones. At least, that's what Chip called them.

"Doesn't explain why he ran." Chip turned his attention to Sandra. "Did Phoenix go to your church?"

"I don't think so. Actually, no, he didn't. I would remember if I'd seen him in church. I never saw him until the softball game."

"What softball game?" Slaughter asked.

"Right here." Sandra pointed her chin in the direction of the softball field, which they couldn't see through the trees. "We have a church team, and we played a game against Grace Evangelical from Livermore Falls on Tuesday."

Slaughter looked irritated at the idea of a church softball team. Sandra found herself caring less and less about Slaughter's irritation levels.

"Did he play for Livermore Falls?" Chip asked.

"No. He played for us for a little bit. We had someone get hurt, and we didn't have enough people—"

"You didn't have enough people?" Chip glanced toward the church building. "Your church is huge. You can't field a softball team?"

"Would you please focus?" Slaughter said, her voice tight.

"Yes, a lot of people do come to church on Sunday morning, and yes, we do have trouble fielding a team." She didn't think she needed to tell him that Brendan Barney continued to scare off potential roster fillers. "So, someone got hurt, and my husband invited Phoenix to play. He was in the bleachers."

"Bleachers? Why was he in the bleachers?"

How was she supposed to know? Although, in the past she had known things that Chip thought she shouldn't have known, so maybe his expectations weren't unwarranted. "I don't know. He was alone. I mean he was sitting with a bunch of people, but it seemed like he'd come to the game alone. And he was certainly all alone when he ran away from the police."

Slaughter's thin eyebrow perked up. "Does your husband know him? Why did he pick him?"

She shook her head, maybe a little too emphatically. "He didn't know him. We were desperate, and he was a man wearing sneakers. If he had said no, my husband would have asked the pastor's wife next."

Without smiling, Chip chuckled. He knew the pastor's wife well enough to know how ridiculous that would be. She was far too mild-mannered to be handling a bat. If given one, she would probably polish it.

"Did he talk to anyone at the game?"

Sandra thought. "I don't think so."

"No one talked to him?"

"Not that I saw. And I think I would have noticed. He was the most interesting thing about the game."

"Well, thank you for your help." Chip swung his arm back toward the church. "You'd better get back inside before the service starts."

Sandra didn't want to go back to church. Her mind scrambled to think of something else to say, something to ask so that she could remain a part of this. "How did he die?" she spat out.

Chip paused. "We don't have an official cause of death yet," he said slowly.

Too late, Sandra realized the stupidity of what she had just asked. It was obvious from the scene that Phoenix had suffered a terrific head injury. The cause of death was that someone had clobbered him. "What I meant to say," she hurried to save face, "is what did they hit him with?" She looked around the forest floor as if she were going to spot a crowbar that all these cops had missed.

"Something big—"

Slaughter interrupted him, "We're not ready to share details of an open investigation. I'm sure you understand."

Much to Sandra's delight, Chip completely ignored Slaughter's redirection. "We haven't found the weapon yet."

Chapter 7

Pastor Cliff shared from the pulpit that he didn't have any details, but that a man had been killed the night before in the woods adjacent to the church's property. Sandra didn't know how he knew it had happened the night before, but she didn't challenge his assumption. They had a moment of silence and then prayed for all those involved. While everyone else had their heads down and their eyes closed, Sandra looked around the sanctuary, not even sure what she was looking for. Was anyone sad? Grieving? Did anyone know the man or appear to care that he was gone? Did anyone look guilty? But no one was racked with sobs, and save for a few rebellious children, no one else had their head raised.

After the prayer and a series of announcements that could have been avoided if people would just read the bulletin, the music started, and everyone stood to sing. During the second verse, Ethel slid into Sandra's row. This was a pleasant surprise. Ethel usually sat in the back with all her senior friends. "What did you find out?" she almost shouted over the music.

"Precious little." Sandra tried not to shout, but she knew Ethel's hearing wasn't the best. "The victim's name is Phoenix Haynes. He was at the softball game on Tuesday, but I don't know him, and I don't know anyone else who knows him." Sandra looked around to see if anyone was listening, but everybody around them appeared to be focusing on their singing. "Someone hit him in the head."

Ethel's wrinkled hand flew to her chest as she gasped appropriately. "Oh my." She knew from experience how unpleasant it was to be thumped over the head.

When Ethel didn't say more, Sandra tried to return to focusing on *her* singing, but it wasn't easy. Her mind was spinning. Should she call on Bob? Of course she should. He would want to know. But maybe he already did know. He was an angel, after all. Angels knew things. And she knew her church had a church angel. Certainly *that* guy was aware of what was going on. Maybe he'd told Bob? Or maybe it was none of Bob's business. Maybe this was above his pay grade.

So, she shouldn't call Bob. But she really wanted to. Would it irritate Bob if she called him? Did he *want* to be beckoned every time she was near a crisis? Maybe she should leave it up to God to assign angels to the world's crises.

She realized she was feeling shy about reaching out to her favorite angel. It had been so long since she'd seen him. Maybe she should just stay out of this one. She didn't know Phoenix. She had no skin in this game. Maybe she should let the police handle it and not get thrown into another trunk or off another snowmobile.

That settled it then. She would stay out of it. Her husband would be grateful.

The sermon stretched on and on. Usually, Pastor Cliff's lessons were short and poignant. And maybe this one was too; maybe she just wasn't getting it. She was too busy thinking about what was going on outside. What if she were the detective? What would be her first move? Find the murder weapon. But she, Sandra Provost, church mom, theater mom, soccer mom, fearless church softball scorekeeper, would not be able to find a murder weapon that fifty cops couldn't find. She didn't see a way that she could be helpful or useful with this one, and she reminded herself that she'd already decided to stay out of it anyway.

With her mind somewhat settled, she tried to concentrate on the sermon. She felt good about her decision. She would focus on the many other parts of her life that needed her attention, and then she wouldn't need to bother Bob. Because if she didn't get herself mixed up in this mystery, then *he* wouldn't need to get mixed up in this mystery. As she tried to follow the pastor's words, she felt as though someone was staring at the back of her head. For several minutes, she fought the urge to turn around and look, but the sensation only grew stronger, and finally she gave in. She tried to be discreet, pretending she was looking at the clock in the back of the room, and what she saw standing under the clock made her face explode into a smile.

There stood Bob, looking at her, his eyes wide as if to ask, "What are you doing in here when there's a murder victim outside?"

Chapter 8

Pretending she needed to go to the bathroom, Sandra left the sanctuary before the service was over and looked around for her oft invisible friend. She found him in the hallway and watched him duck into the dark library. She followed him inside and flicked on the light. She wondered why he'd chosen the library, but then realized no one ever used the room, and he probably knew that.

"Nice to see you!" She ignored her urge to give him a big hug.

"You as well. I'm afraid I have some bad news."

Her stomach tightened. "What?"

"I can't help you with this investigation."

She wasn't sure what to say. Part of her was devastated. Part of her didn't believe him. "Why?"

He folded his arms across his chest. "Let's just say that the powers that be weren't very happy with my little jaunt out to the theater last winter."

"The powers that be? You mean God?"

He didn't agree, and she took this as disagreement. "I can't say."

Of course he couldn't. "Did you get into trouble?" She really hoped this hadn't been the case. She didn't want that on her conscience.

"Not exactly. But I don't *want* to get in trouble, so I'm sorry, I have to sit this one out. That's not to say that you can't pray for help if you get into a pinch. I'm sure God will send someone."

A lump formed in her throat. Was this really happening?

"Besides, you don't need me. You do most of the work on your own anyway. I just push old men out of bogs."

She snickered. "You do a lot more than that, and you know it. But, I think, under the circumstances, I should sit this one out too."

"That's probably wise." He nodded awkwardly. "Okay, well I've got to get back to work."

"You don't get to rest on Sundays?" She didn't want him to leave.

"I do, but there are a lot of sports camps going on right now, and every coach thinks his or her sport is the only sport their kids play in the summer." He took a deep breath. "They keep me busier in the summer than during the actual seasons."

She was grateful that Peter only played one sport. Summer soccer took up enough of their time without adding another demanding coach to their schedule. She didn't know what else to say. "All right then. I still hope to see you again?"

"Oh, I'm sure you will." He didn't sound convincing. He hesitated and then stepped forward and gave her the hug she'd been wanting to give him since she'd seen him under the clock.

And then, before she'd even let go, he vanished, and tears sprang to her eyes. She wiped them away quickly. It was silly to cry over this. He was an angel. He couldn't be her best friend. They couldn't just hang out whenever she wanted. He had a supernatural schedule to stick to. She turned the light off and left the library, trying to be grateful that she'd gotten to spend as much time with him as she had.

By the time she got back to the sanctuary, people were spilling out of it. She was glad. She was no longer in the mood for church. She just wanted to be alone.

Peter caught her eye. "We're staying for the potluck, right?"

Oh no. She'd completely forgotten about it. "Sorry, I forgot there was a potluck, and I didn't bring anything—"

"Not to worry!" Ethel materialized beside her. "I brought enough for four families! Come on downstairs and relax!"

Sandra didn't *want* to go downstairs. Church potlucks were the opposite of relaxing. She wanted to go home and grieve in solitude.

"Please?" Peter begged. At least he *wanted* to hang out at church now. There was a time when that hadn't been the case. But lately Peter had grown more popular with the ladies.

Nate came up behind Peter. "Did we bring anything for the potluck?"

Sandra restrained her eye roll. Had he *seen* her sneak a casserole into the minivan this morning?

"*I* brought your family's contribution, so let's get downstairs before all the good stuff is gone!"

Grudgingly, Sandra followed Ethel down into the basement fellowship hall.

"Why don't you want to stay?" Nate asked. "Were you planning on starting your investigation immediately?"

She didn't like his tone. "There isn't going to be any investigation," she snapped and then made a beeline for the deviled eggs, wondering why some church potluck enthusiast hadn't renamed them angeled eggs by now.

Chapter 9

The summer days flew by: swimming lessons, soccer practices, softball games—it was a blur. Yet, Sandra still made time to watch the news and check the internet news sites. But there was no word about the man who'd been found dead in the Plainfield woods. She'd even bought the paper—because the grocery store clerk had given Sandra the hairy eyeball when she'd tried to read it standing beside the newsstand—but nothing. Either the police were really good at keeping secrets, they weren't progressing much in their investigation, or they weren't *trying* to progress in their investigation. Maybe they were too busy. Their kids had soccer camps too. Whatever the reason, it was driving Sandra crazy. A man had been killed, for crying out loud. She couldn't stand not knowing who had killed him and why.

When she ran into Detective Slaughter in the potato chip aisle at Shop 'n Save, she was certain the meeting was the product of divine intervention. "Hello!" she sang out with too much cheer.

Slaughter managed to not snarl, but just barely. "Hello." She quickly turned her attention back to the multiple flavors of kettle cooked chips.

"I recommend the sour cream and onion."

"I hate onions."

Of course she did. "Oh, sorry to hear that. I'm afraid they don't make them with just sour cream." She tee-heed nervously, and Sammy gave her a worried look from his shopping cart perch. She reached for a bag of the aforementioned sour cream and onion even though she'd originally had no intention of buying them. She was so nervous she didn't know what her hands were doing. "How goes the investigation?" She tried to sound casual and failed.

"I'm not discussing that with you," Slaughter said, barely opening her mouth. She would make a great ventriloquist, except that ventriloquists were funny.

"Does that mean there's actually something to discuss?" Sandra allowed her frustration to ring through the words.

Slaughter's eyes snapped toward Sandra. "What is that supposed to mean?"

"I mean," Sandra said slowly, "that according to the news, there doesn't seem to be much investigating in this investigation."

Slaughter's lips parted just a hair, and for a second, Sandra feared she was going to hiss at her. But instead, words came out. "I know you think you have a clue, but you don't. I'm knee-deep in unsolved cases, and we're not going to spend all our time on one homeless man." Without looking, she snatched a bag of kettle cooked sour cream and onion potato chips with such force that the crunching sound served as a fitting exclamation point to her statement. Then she spun on her heel and stomped away, her unwanted oniony chips in one hand and her empty shopping basket in the other.

What a fearsome woman, Sandra thought. She put her own bag of unwanted potato chips back on the shelf and grabbed the cheesy tortilla chips that the rest of her family would eat. She tossed them into her cart, though it was more like tossing them *onto* her cart, as it was already brimming over with both staples and sweets. Staring at the bag of chips perched on the mountaintop, she had two thoughts. One, how much was this going to cost? And two, Slaughter had only carried an empty basket. Maybe she didn't have a family. Maybe she didn't have anyone. A pang of sadness stabbed at Sandra's chest. Then she reminded herself that Slaughter had suggested she cared less about finding Phoenix's killer because he was homeless, and then she didn't feel so bad for Slaughter.

She headed for the checkout, and then checked the clock every thirty seconds as she waited in line. It was almost time to pick up Joanna from soccer, and she didn't want to be late. She didn't want to scare Joanna, and she didn't want to burden the volunteer coaches with after-practice childcare that they'd never signed up for. She bounced up and down, and Sammy caught her anxiety and began to cry. This made the cashier work faster, and soon it was Sandra's turn to give the store all her money.

With her wallet empty and her cart full of bagged groceries, she headed out into the hot sun. Unloading the cart into the back of her van made her miss Peter, who usually did this for her, but he was at a friend's house, unfortunately. She wiped the sweat away from her eyes as she returned the cart to its corral, and then she scooped Sammy out of it so she could buckle him into the sizzling hot van. He screamed in protest and she tried to comfort him, but what was there to say? It was going to be mighty uncomfortable until she got the A/C going.

Five minutes later, the heat's brutality had been pushed out by the cold air blowing out of her dashboard, and Sammy was either happy or asleep. She didn't know which, and it didn't matter.

She pulled into the school parking lot with several minutes to spare. She saw Nate's car in his designated principal parking spot. Though he didn't need to be there during summer school hours, he usually made sure that he was. Should she pop in and see her husband or recline the seat and relax for five minutes? She put her hand on the recline lever and Sammy started crying. Visit the hubbie it was.

Nate's face lit up when he saw her, and she breezed into his office praising his air conditioning. Only once she was inside did she see he had a student there with him. "Oh! Hello," she said awkwardly, a little embarrassed that she'd been that excited about cold air.

He gave her a half smile but didn't say anything.

"Mrs. Provost, this is Adam. Adam, this is my lovely wife."

Adam looked at the floor.

"Nice to meet you, Adam."

He did not look up.

She didn't take it personally. First, he was in summer school. Then, he was in the principal's office. He probably wasn't having a good day. "Well, I just came to pick up Joanna. I just thought we'd say hi. Don't forget you've got a softball game tonight." She turned to go.

"Hey, what a great idea!" he exclaimed.

What? Had she had an idea? She turned back.

"How do you feel about softball?" Nate was looking at Adam.

Adam shrugged. "I like it, I guess."

"Excellent! Because we need some more players. Why don't you come play for us? Game starts at six, but we start throwing the ball around at five-thirty."

Adam didn't look convinced.

"Come on, it'll be fun."

"Can my brothers come?"

Nate hesitated. Sandra didn't think Adam would be able to read this hesitation, but it was clear to her that whoever Adam's brothers were, Nate didn't really want them to come. "Sure! The more the merrier!"

Chapter 10

Adam showed up in the church parking lot at five-thirty sharp. He came bouncing in, along with two other young men, in the back of a stove-up Toyota pickup. Sandra assumed they were Adam's brothers. Then two more men spilled out of the cab. Or maybe *those* were the brothers. She looked at the field. Pastor Cliff was there, of course, along with Richard and Brendan Barney, Boomer, Nate, and Loriana, the sole female representation for the day. Six originals plus five newcomers meant they could field a team with a sub to spare. She flashed Nate a delighted smile, but it fell from her face when she saw his expression. Why did he look so nervous?

At first, no one spoke to the guests, but something jerked Nate into action and his face sprang into diplomat mode with a broad smile. "Welcome! So glad you could come!" He began shaking hands and introducing himself and the others. The men grabbed balls out of the bucket and walked out onto the field. They started tossing the balls back and forth, notably *not* playing with any of the originals, but this was to be expected, wasn't it? There was an even number of them. It would be weird if they mingled right away.

Nate plopped down beside her on the bench and made a silly face at Sammy.

"What's wrong?" she muttered.

"Nothing," he said through closed teeth. "I invited him to play because I was trying to get him *away* from his family. Now he's just brought them all along."

"What's wrong with them?"

He looked at her as if he didn't quite dare to tell her. "They're *Bickfords*."

"Oh!" Now she understood his nerves. "It'll be fine," she tried to comfort him. "This is a ministry, remember?"

He nodded. "I remember." He still didn't open his mouth.

"Besides, if they cause too much trouble, I'll just call the town cops, and they'll come chase them into the woods."

Laughter burst out of Nate, finally forcing him to open his mouth. He tipped his head back and laughed toward the clouds. Then he kissed her on the cheek. "Thanks. I needed that. And you're right. I'm sure it will be fine." He patted her on the leg and then went to greet Lewis, who had just arrived.

Joanna began pulling the bats out of the bat bag.

"Careful, honey!" New Hope Church was the proud owner of a profoundly useless collection of old softball bats. The rubber had worn or peeled off several of the bat handles, and had been repaired with athletic tape that had yellowed and frayed over the years. These bats had the logos worn off them, and Sandra couldn't understand why they didn't just throw them away, but they'd been donated by someone at some point and no one wanted to step on any toes, so for every practice and every game, someone hauled them out of the closet and schlepped them down to the field. Richard and Brendan brought their own bats, of course, bragging about how much they'd cost and how much they would help them hit—which they never did. Boomer brought his own bat too, but he was quick to say he'd gotten it for a steal at Marden's Surplus and Salvage. And everyone else used a bat that someone had donated last year that still had its handle and its logo. The rest just stayed in the bag—unless Joanna took them out of the bag.

She dropped the last bat with a clang and then looked satisfied, as if she'd done something to help.

"Good job. Now you can put them all back."

"Really?" She obviously didn't like this directive.

"Really." Sandra glanced at the old bats, which Joanna had lined up neatly across the center of the dugout. Before she became consciously aware of what she was seeing, the bottom dropped out of her stomach. Joanna reached down to grab a bat. "Joanna, stop!" Sandra said too sharply. She stood up and grabbed her daughter, the scorebook falling off her lap and into the dirt. She pulled Joanna away and then stepped closer to the bats and looked down. It couldn't be. But it was. One of the bats was covered in a dark red that could only be blood. She pulled Joanna toward the dugout's exit. "Go get your father."

"What's wrong, Mommy?"

"Go get him now!" She pushed Joanna out of the dugout and then reached for her purse, scrambling to get the phone out. She started to dial 911 and then thought better of it and went back into the purse for her wallet. Because somewhere in there, among a million diaper coupons and loyalty punch cards that never got filled, she had Chip Buker's card. She found it and dialed his number as Nate stepped into the dugout. Wordlessly, she pointed out the bloody bat for her husband. Then, "Hi? Chip? It's Sandra Provost. Can you come to the church? I think I just found the murder weapon."

Chapter 11

Detective Chip Buker arrived with an entourage. Sandra showed him to the suspect bat and then he promptly had her escorted away. Despite her awareness that this was probably correct protocol, she was still offended. He made her stand a hundred feet away from the dugout—as if she was just an ordinary civilian. She stood with her arms folded across her chest glaring at him, further annoyed that he wasn't paying enough attention to even notice her glares.

"You okay?" Nate asked, slipping his arm around her waist.

"No. He's going to make us late." It was quarter after six, and some of the Bickfords were staring longingly at their pickup.

"That's okay. We've got plenty of daylight."

She didn't appreciate his patience. "The Bickfords are going to leave."

He snorted. "Since when did you care about the Bickfords?"

"Since always." This wasn't true. She'd never really thought about them one way or the other, though they were frequently the talk of the town. The sprawling family lived in the woods of Plainfield, in an area the locals had coined the Bickford Block. They all lived on Mink Brook Road, which was a narrow dirt road that ran in three equal lengths to form a square with Route 27. The many Bickfords lived in small houses or trailers all along this road. They were often in trouble, and a few of them were currently "away" serving time. She looked up at her husband. "Since when did *you* care about the Bickfords?"

"What do you mean?"

"I mean, you inviting Adam to a church softball game. Quite a risk for a public school principal to take, don't you think?"

"Nah. I didn't invite him to church. It's just a fun outdoor activity to keep him out of trouble."

"And is he in trouble a lot?"

Nate nodded. "You know I can't say much. But I like Adam. I want to see him succeed."

This didn't surprise her. As far as she knew, Nate liked all of his students. One of the Bickfords headed for the truck. *Oh for heaven's sake.* She stomped toward Chip, who was supervising as the slowest investigators in the world wrapped the bat bag in an enormous sheet of plastic.

Without looking at her, he said, "I can't tell you anything."

"I'm not here to ask about the investigation. I'm here to tell you that you need to let us get on with the softball game."

He gave her an incredulous look. "There's been a murder," he said slowly, "and we've just found the murder weapon—"

Actually, she was pretty sure *she'd* found the weapon, but she would let that slide in the interest of time.

—"and you're worried about starting a church softball game on time?"

She stepped closer to him, now inside the off-limits dugout. "This is a ministry," she said, her voice so low he had to lean toward her to hear, "and the people we are trying to minister to are leaving." She allowed her voice to come back to normal volume. "We won't use the dugout. We won't come near you. Just let us start the game."

Chip glanced around the field, which was now peppered with people playing catch or just standing around. He nodded, his jaw tight. "Fine. Go ahead."

"Great. Thank you." She looked around for the umpire, but he was nowhere to be seen. Oh no, had he left? She trotted back to Nate. "Where did the ump go?"

"I think he's in his truck." He turned to scan the parking lot.

"Well, go get him. Chip said we can play. We've just got to stay out of the dugout."

"Great! Good job!" He squeezed her shoulder. "I'll go let him know. Let's just use the front row of the bleachers for a dugout."

"Yep. And you're all going to have to use Boomer's bat. I doubt Richard or Brendan are going to share theirs."

Nate snickered and jogged away from her.

She headed toward the Bickfords' truck, which was now running. "Don't leave yet!" she called out from fifty feet away. "We're going to start!"

The man behind the wheel nodded to her, shut off the engine, and climbed back out of the truck. "Didn't mean to be unpatient," he said, with a partly toothless smile, "but cops make me nervous."

She smiled, even though he was now making *her* nervous. "I understand."

"I hear you guys had a killing here, huh?"

Oh boy. "Yes, sadly, we did."

"But that's not a normal thing, right? People who play softball for you don't get offed if they miss a catch?"

Despite herself, she had to laugh at that. "Definitely not. We never catch anything, so we wouldn't have anyone left to play."

He thought this was hysterical and hooted so loudly his voice echoed. As he walked by her toward the field, she caught a whiff of beer and wondered if she'd misunderstood why he was sitting in his truck. If he'd indulged in a few pre-game nips, that might make the game more interesting.

Ton Truck Bickford offered to pitch. She didn't know what his real name was, but the nickname fit. She'd never use it out loud, of course, but his family members didn't seem worried about hurting his feelings.

Pastor Cliff could have been more tactful when he told Ton Truck that no, *he* was the pitcher.

Ton Truck argued that he was "wicked fast," but Pastor would not be moved.

Sandra had never had cause to wonder about Pastor's pitching, but now that Ton Truck had brought it up, she muttered to Nate, "Why *does* Pastor always pitch? It's not like he's that great at it."

Even though she'd been very quiet with her question, Nate shushed her. Then he answered her through closed teeth, "He says it's to keep people from fighting over the position." This didn't make any sense, and Nate gave her a look that said he was aware of that senselessness. But she also knew he wouldn't ruffle any feathers unless he had to. Nate was a peacekeeper.

Ton Truck made his discontent clear as he trudged toward his assigned position at second base. As he punctuated his complaints with a few choice curse words, several players from Jay Baptist stared at him in horror. Oh dear, the Bickfords were going to do a number on New Hope's reputation.

Jay Baptist's first batter pounded it toward left field. Sandra had no doubt that it would be a home run. It looked as though it was going to fall just shy of the Purple Monster. Years ago, some Red Sox fans had erected a tall plywood wall in left field and had painted it green in honor of their favorite pro baseball stadium. Some years since, after the green paint had faded, chipped, and fell away, some well-meaning church servants had repainted the wall with purple paint leftover from a Vacation Bible School play. Some people were furious. The Red Sox tribute didn't work if the wall was purple. But some people, including Sandra, found it hysterical and were proud to have a Purple Monster in left field.

She hadn't been watching the left fielder. She'd been watching the ball. So she almost fell off the bleachers in shock when a wiry Bickford suddenly appeared under the ball and caught it before it hit the ground. It wasn't the first run for Jay Baptist. It was the first out for New Hope.

She'd never witnessed anything so incredible in her life, and she'd hung out with an angel.

Chapter 12

New Hope Church scored seven runs in the bottom of the first inning, thanks entirely to four of the six Bickfords. It was more runs than they'd scored all season combined, yet Sandra seemed to be the only one cheering. The spectators in the bleachers were peculiarly somber. She wanted to blame it on the fact that someone had been killed in the adjacent woods, and that they'd just found a bloody bat in their bat bag, but she didn't think that was it. She was afraid they were uncomfortable that the local riffraff had invaded their softball club.

At this thought, something clicked in her mind. Some might consider Phoenix to have been riffraff too. Maybe he had traveled in some of the same circles as the Bickfords? She shook her head. She wasn't supposed to be thinking about that. She wasn't going to get involved with this one.

Jay Baptist pounded the ball in all directions, but if it went near a Bickford, it got scooped up and thrown to first, where Boomer always caught it. Hence, New Hope had two outs before Jay Baptist had scored a run. But then Jay's coach caught on. "You've got to hit it toward short!" he called out. "Keep it on the ground!" In other words, he'd noticed that New Hope had an old man playing shortstop, and that old man was absolutely terrible at fielding the ball. If Jay hit it to first base, second base, or anywhere in the outfield, chances were good that the Bickfords or Boomer would catch it. But this was not the case at shortstop. That coach must have wondered why on earth New Hope was playing such a dud at short when they obviously had so many good players. Or maybe he'd been playing church softball long enough to know exactly what was going on.

Jay's players did exactly what they were told; they hit two grounders to short, and got two men on base. But when the third batter in a row hit the ball to shortstop again, out of nowhere, the Bickford in left field appeared in the dirt beside Richard Barney, essentially stole his play from him, and then threw the ball to third to get the final out—except that it was Richard's son playing third base, and he was so appalled at the dishonor that had been done to his father that he didn't even attempt to tag the bag. He caught the ball, sure, but then he just held it in his glove as he stomped toward the offending Bickford.

Sandra couldn't hear what Brendan Barney said, but she saw him poke the Bickford in the chest and she braced herself for what she feared was coming. Sure enough, the Bickford drew back and then swung his fist at Brendan's pretty little face. It appeared that Brendan did not know it was coming, as he made no move to dodge the blow, and was suddenly lying on his side in the dirt.

"Run!" the Jay coach called to his man on third. He was such an opportunist. The runner on third started for home, but the umpire waved him off, called time out, and told him to go back to his base. Then he took off his mask and headed toward the commotion, where two Bickfords held their boxing cousin back from the man on the ground, who didn't seem in any hurry to get up. He was squirming a lot, so Sandra knew he was alive.

In a move that surprised no one, the umpire threw the boxer out of the game. But then he also ejected Brendan Barney, and this did *not* go well with Pops at shortstop, who started screaming into the umpire's face. Looking almost amused, the umpire then threw him out also, and just like that, New Hope was down to a reduced lineup again. Sandra wondered if the rest of the Bickfords would leave, but they didn't. The boxer went and sat in the truck, where there were probably refreshments, and the rest of them spread out across the field as if this sort of thing happened to them all the time.

The next Jay batter hit it to shortstop again, which was no longer a wise decision. The Bickford who had moved in from centerfield easily threw the batter out, and it was New Hope's turn to bat again.

Once Sandra got the scorebook caught up, she pretended she needed to stretch her legs and approached the Bickford she'd earlier rousted out of his pickup. "Well, that was certainly exciting!" She cringed at her own pathetic attempt to make small talk.

He spit into the dirt and she realized he had a chaw in. *That* wasn't going to go over well with church leadership. As if any of this was. She wondered if they'd kick her husband out of the church for all this.

"I'm Sandra, Nate's wife." She wanted to learn his name, but she wanted to be clear she wasn't flirting.

He nodded, squinting in the early evening slanting sunlight. "The principal?"

She nodded. "Yep! That's right." *Stop sounding so chipper, Sandra. It's weird.*

He nodded again but looked away from her.

"Lineup!" Lewis hollered.

Beyond annoyed, she looked down at the book and then hollered out the lineup. Then she looked at the man beside her. "And what's your name?"

"Danny."

"Nice to meet you, Danny. You guys sure do seem to be good at softball. We're glad to have you. This is the first lead we've had all season."

"Yeah ..." He sounded bored with this conversation. "Well, we play a lot."

They must. "You do?"

"Yeah, in the men's league. We're on a few different teams. This is our first church team, though." He spit again.

"Well, welcome. You know, you mentioned the guy who died. Did you know him?"

His head snapped toward her, and he scowled down at her, his bushy eyebrows smashed together. "No, why?"

She shrugged, backing away a little.

"No reason. Just trying to make conversation."

Danny seemed to accept this. "Nah, I never heard of 'im. He wasn't from around here."

Chapter 13

Thanks to the Bickfords, New Hope got their first notch in the win column.

"Did Pastor say anything to you about your new friends?" Sandra asked, once they were all safely ensconced in the minivan and pointed toward home.

Nate laughed. "No, thank goodness. They really were good, weren't they?"

"Yep. I think we should keep them."

Nate tightened his grip on the steering wheel. "Not sure that's going to happen."

She didn't know what that meant. Was he worried they wouldn't want to come back or did he think someone was going to tell them to stay away?

"They were something, though," Nate said thoughtfully. "They looked like a bunch of wild animals, but they played like ... well, like wild animals, but in a good way."

"That's not very nice, Daddy," Joanna scolded.

"You're right. I'm sorry. I didn't mean it to be mean. I just meant ..." *Just quit while you're ahead.*

"Do you really think that was the murder weapon?" he asked.

She chewed her lip. "I do. I can't imagine why else there would be dried blood on a bat no one has used in years.

"Do you know what this means?"

She had a few ideas, but she didn't know what *he* thought it meant. "No, what?"

He glanced away from the road to give her a grave look. Then he said, so quietly she almost couldn't hear him, "It means it was one of us."

"Oh no," she said quickly, "not necessarily."

"Yes, necessarily! How else would someone have access to our bats? We keep them in the *church!*"

"Yeah, but we also keep them lying out in the open all the time, and we sometimes forget to put them away. Someone could have grabbed a bat while the bag was open and unattended somewhere—"

"And then that stranger snuck into the church to put the bat back?" He looked at her again to convey his doubt. "Highly unlikely. There's only so many people with a church key."

He was making sense, and she didn't like the sound of it. First, the idea of someone from their church being the murderer made her stomach roll. Second, she didn't like her husband being better at the puzzle solving than she was. Why hadn't she realized it had to be someone from the church? Maybe because she didn't *want* to think that?

"So either someone unlocked the church to put the bat back that night, or they snuck it in later the next day or on another day. Either way, it's not good."

She was quiet as that soaked in.

"Maybe they didn't have a key," Peter said.

Oh great. Now her son was doing it too.

"Maybe someone broke into the church," he added. "People leave doors and windows unlocked all the time."

"That's an excellent point," Nate said. "But it still doesn't point to a stranger. If you weren't familiar with our church and you needed a murder weapon, you wouldn't go searching for our bat bag. There are easier ways to find a weapon—"

"Guys!" Sandra cried, exasperated.

"What?" Nate looked so innocent.

"You tell me I can't get involved with this, and now here you are trying to figure it out!"

"We're just talking," Nate said, sounding injured. "We're not chasing bad guys into a forest during a snowstorm. There's no harm in talking—"

"Well, cut it out. I feel like a drug addict trying to stay away from the drugs, and now you guys are using right in front of me."

At first, no one said anything. Then Peter said, "I think that's an exaggeration."

"I made my point," she snapped. She wasn't really angry at them, though. They were just *really* making her miss Bob. She wanted to talk to *him* about all this. He helped her process this stuff. Though, thinking about him gave her an idea. She glanced nervously at Nate, having this odd fear that he could read her mind, but he looked clueless. So, she stayed silent all the way home, and she didn't talk as she put the frozen pizzas in the oven. Then she approached Nate, who was sitting on the couch watching television, from behind, kissed him on the top of the head and whispered, "Would you mind getting the pizzas out of the oven in twenty? I set the timer."

He craned his neck around to look at her. "Why? Where are you going?"

She leaned on the back of the couch. "I just want to go for a drive," she sort-of lied. "I'm not hungry."

His eyes narrowed. "Are you going to meet Bob?"

She snorted. "No, I promise. I'm not going to meet Bob. He quit crime-fighting, remember?"

He didn't look convinced. "I remember."

She kissed him on the cheek and then stood up straight. "I promise, no angels, and no chasing anyone into the forest. I'm just going for a drive."

"Okay, then." His tone suggested it was not okay at all. "But will you call and check in? I'll worry."

"I won't need to. I won't be gone long."

He frowned.

"Okay, I'll call and check in." She said good-bye and then sneaked out before her kids could notice she was leaving them and freak out. Then as she slid out the door, she reached up and grabbed Nate's keys off the hook. She'd said she was going for a drive. She hadn't specified with which vehicle.

Chapter 14

S andra slid Nate's church key into the lock and then slipped into the cool, dark, empty building. She'd never trespassed before and felt extra guilty that her first foray into the crime was a church—her *own* church, no less. She fervently hoped the church angel wasn't watching. Did it count as breaking and entering if she didn't steal anything? She feared so. It was a moot point, however, because if she found what she was looking for, she planned to take it.

She knew from general church scuttlebutt that the master key that unlocked the outside door also unlocked most of the doors in the building, except for the pastor's office and the treasurer's office. That was okay. She didn't think she needed to go into either of those rooms. She gave her eyes time to adjust to the dim light provided by the emergency exit signs and then headed for the secretary's office door. In seconds she was inside. Thank goodness Nate frequently volunteered for youth group activities; this mission would be far more difficult without his key. She looked around the neat but cluttered office. She quickly spotted the small television screen, which was turned off, but she didn't see a box of tapes anywhere. Maybe she'd been watching too many old detective shows. Maybe New Hope's security footage was digital. She groaned, which sounded freakily loud in the silence. She continued her search, but as the tapes didn't appear, she grew more and more sure that there were no tapes. She turned to confront the secretary's computer. Sandra wasn't a computer whiz. Was it even worth turning it on?

She hadn't come this far to just give up. She looked for the computer's on button and learned that it already was on. It was just sleeping. She jiggled the ergonomically-correct mouse and the screen sprang to life, blinding her with its brightly lit password request. *Shoot.* But then she saw a combination of letters and numbers taped to the bottom of the computer screen. No way it could be that easy?

But it was. She was soon inside the belly of all things New Hope. Sunday school curricula, bulletin templates, and schedules galore. The desktop was full of icons, one of which read "Cameras." She opened the file folder and found several thousand video files stretching back years. That was a lot of empty parking lot footage. She was beyond grateful to learn the files were organized by date, and she quickly scrolled down to locate the footage from that fateful Saturday night. Then she scrolled back up. Then down. It wasn't there. There was a video for Friday and the following Monday, but nothing for that Saturday or Sunday. She scanned the other dates to see if missing videos was a common occurrence, but it wasn't. On a hunch, she checked for the Tuesday when she'd first seen Phoneix, and that recording was missing too. That couldn't be a coincidence. Someone had deleted three days' worth of footage? Who could have done that?

Anyone could have done it. She'd just proved that their church wasn't exactly Fort Knox. It occurred to her that she could delete the current day's footage that showed her sneaking into the church after dark, but she decided she'd crossed enough ethical lines for one day. She closed the folder, hoped the computer would go back to sleep soon, and then sneaked out of the office, taking care to lock the door behind her. Then she was outside, making sure she didn't look directly at the security cameras and hurrying to Nate's car, which she'd parked out of their view. And then she was on her way home, her small guilt about what she'd just done completely dwarfed by her curiosity. She'd assumed that the police hadn't asked for the videos, but maybe they had? But even if they had, that didn't mean they would have been *deleted*, did it? Wouldn't they just have copied the videos? No, she was sure the police hadn't yet asked for the videos. They'd only just taken custody of the bats that evening, so unless they'd had another reason to suspect the killer was someone from the church, she doubted they'd made the leap yet.

She resisted the urge to swing through the Dunkin drive through for a sweet treat and was almost back to her driveway when Bob appeared in the seat beside her. She shrieked, and the car swerved toward the ditch as she stared at him.

"Keep it on the road!" he cried, bracing himself with one hand on the dash.

She straightened the car out and then opened her mouth to ask him why he was trying to kill her, but before she could speak, he told her to pull over.

"Pull over? You just told me to keep it on the road!"

"Pull over right now!"

She slowed and pulled the car onto the dirt shoulder. It always made her nervous when he injected his voice with angel authority.

Chapter 15

"Are you out of your mind?" Bob cried.

"What?" She didn't know what he meant. Surely he couldn't be this wound up about her sneaking into her own church?

"You broke into a church!"

"How do you know? Have you been spying on me?"

She might as well have suggested he'd spent the last several hours crocheting doilies. Spying on her was obviously beneath him. "Certainly not. Mannaziah told me to come rebuke you, and he's acting as though it is my fault that you are behaving like this."

"Who is Mannaziah?"

He flinched. He'd said too much. "Your church angel," he muttered. "But that is not important right now. You can't go breaking into the church."

"I didn't *break* in, Bob. Don't you think you're being a touch dramatic? I had a key."

"Sandra!" He sounded exasperated. "You said you were going to sit this one out."

"And I have! I mean, I did! Until my seven-year-old found the murder weapon!"

His eyes widened. "What? Tell me what happened!"

She told him, and he hung on her every word. He'd obviously missed this too. "Wow," he said when she'd finished.

"And there's more. I wanted to look at the security tapes, only there aren't any actual tapes, but anyway, I tried to watch the videos, but they weren't there—"

"You mean someone deleted them?"

I would tell you if you'd stop interrupting. "Yes, I think someone deleted them. Bob, I think someone from our church killed that man! Do you understand how horrible that is? I mean, I don't know everyone who goes to church there, but I still find it pretty difficult to believe. And whoever did it returned a bloody bat to the bat bag! Who does that? Why not wipe it off first—"

"Unless he was trying to *frame* someone from your church."

She gasped. "You're right! Maybe that *is* the case!"

"Or maybe that's just wishful thinking."

She didn't know, and it was killing her. "So someone took the bat out of the church, walked into the woods with it, clobbered a man, then brought the bat all the way back to the church, put it in the bat bag, and then deleted the video of them doing all this." She looked at him. "That murderer has a lot of intestinal fortitude!"

He stared straight ahead at the dark road in front of them. "Or they're just plain evil."

"Or that." She took a deep breath and exhaled slowly. "Bob, I hate to do this, but I have to get home. I promised my husband that I *wasn't* sneaking out to meet you."

Bob chuckled. "All right. I don't want to get you into trouble, but ..." He didn't finish.

"Yes?"

"Well, I promised Mannaziah that I would get you to stop the investigating, and I'm not confident I've done that. Instead, you've managed to get me intrigued."

"Does this Mannaziah know who killed Phoenix?"

Bob didn't answer her.

"Oh my goodness, he does, doesn't he? Well, can't he just tell you and then you can tell me and then I can tell Chip?" Her voice reached an embarrassingly high pitch by the end of that sentence.

"I don't know if he knows. He wouldn't tell me if he did."

"But he probably does, right?"

"I don't know. Angels don't usually meddle in human affairs as much as I do. I've been a bad example for you." He sounded so discouraged, so vulnerable, that she couldn't stand it.

"Bob, you are the best angel ever."

He snickered.

"I mean it. Otis would be dead if it weren't for you."

He nodded and studied his hands, which were folded in his lap. "Maybe. Or maybe without my meddling, he never would have been in that bog in the first place." He looked up at her. "I'll let you go now."

She opened her mouth to say goodbye, but he was already gone. She took a moment to calm herself down and then drove the rest of the way home, trying to imagine which of her church friends could be a killer. She pictured them in her mind, one by one. Each deacon, each elder, each Sunday school teacher. She pictured the pianist, the base player, and the drummer. She paused on the drummer's face. He was a maybe—always seemed a bit shady. She pictured her friends and Ethel's friends and then laughed out loud. She couldn't picture any of the senior saints swinging a bat—wait. Was she certain that the bats had been in the church when the murderer had picked out his weapon? As she'd told Nate, they hadn't always been put away. She tried to think back—who had dealt with the bat bag that Tuesday? She'd been so busy watching the police chase Phoenix into the woods that she couldn't summon up an image of someone picking up after the team.

She pulled into her driveway and hurried inside, suddenly exhausted. She tried to be discreet as she returned the keys to their hook and then she sank into the couch beside her husband, who hadn't moved since she'd left him.

"I was thinking ..."

He didn't respond.

"Do you have any idea who put the bats away after that Tuesday game where Phoenix helped us out?"

He scratched his chin and then said, "Yeah."

"Well? Who was it?"

He turned his head, and because he was slouched down, he was perfectly eye level with her. "It was me."

Chapter 16

For the first time ever, Sandra was worried the cops might be suspicious of *her*. Apparently, her husband had been the last to handle the bat bag before the murder. And then she'd gone and broken into a church. *Not cool, Sandra, not cool.* The more she tried to tell herself not to worry, the more she worried.

Though she was in bed before ten o'clock, when the alarm went off at six, she'd slept less than two hours. She dragged her body out of bed, her anxiety momentarily displaced by a single overwhelming thought: coffee.

With a half a cup of creamy java in her belly, she sat at the kitchen table and waited for it to make her smarter.

It didn't, and yet she was still able to come to a decision: she needed to confess. She dug through her purse until she found Chip's number, and this time she added him as a contact. If she was going to call him this frequently, she might as well have him on speed dial. She started to call and then realized it was probably too early. So she finished the pot and puttered around the kitchen watching the clock. She took a long shower, almost nodded off under the hot water, and then put on one of her church dresses, specifically, the one she thought made her look the least like a murderer.

Finally, it was eight o'clock, and she decided not to wait for nine. A man had been murdered. If Chip wasn't up yet, he should be.

He was. At least, he answered on the first ring and sounded perky. He was reluctant to meet her in person. He didn't understand why she couldn't just say her piece over the phone, but she persisted. And so, for the first time, she was invited to the Major Crimes Unit office. She left a note for Nate, telling him she was going to see Chip, but not to worry, and that he was in charge of the children until further notice. She planned to get home before he got up and saw the note.

She pulled into the small parking lot less than a half hour later, her hands trembling. She *really* wished Bob were there. He probably wouldn't allow himself to be seen by the detectives, but she'd still like to have him along for moral support. But he wasn't there—at least not to her knowledge—so she dug deep and approached the office one nervous step at a time.

An ice-cold receptionist made her anxiety even worse, but then Chip breezed out into the small lobby, and his sincere welcome put her mostly at ease. He invited her back into his office, and though the two desks in the room suggested he shared the room with Slaughter, she was nowhere in sight. He pulled Slaughter's chair over near his desk. "Have a seat, Sandra. I was just thinking about how well you're doing staying out of this one, and then you called." He chuckled as he folded his hands in his lap. "So, what's up?"

She sat in Slaughter's chair and then swallowed hard. "I have a small confession to make."

He waited for her to say more, but she was at a loss for where to begin. "Okay." He drew out the second syllable far too long.

She needed to jump right in. She took a deep breath and then let loose. "So I know that I shouldn't have, but I got to thinking about who had access to that bat, and so I thought it had to be someone from my church, and then I thought, hey, we have security cameras around the church, because about eight years ago we had some vandalism ..." She gasped for more air and then kept going. "Anyway, so the cameras aren't everywhere, but I knew there was one over the door, so I snuck into the church at night and checked the videos from the security cameras, but the videos from the day of the softball game, the day that Phoenix ran into the woods, and the day of his murder, and the day *after* his murder—all those videos are gone." She gave him about a second and a half to respond to that before asking, "And you didn't take them, right?"

He shifted in his chair. "When does the confession start?"

Huh? "That was the confession."

He furrowed his brow. "What, that you snuck into church?"

Suddenly, she felt very small and very silly. "Yes. And because I interfered with your investigation."

He blew out a puff of air. "That's okay. I don't want you to make a habit of it, but to be honest, we hadn't gotten to the church's cameras yet."

She got the distinct impression he'd had no plans to ever get to those cameras.

"Well, I just wanted you to know that I didn't delete them."

"And I didn't delete them."

"But someone did."

He nodded contemplatively. "And we need to find out who."

She wanted to offer a suggestion, but didn't want to step on his toes. "So maybe we should fingerprint the secretary's office?"

His eyebrows flicked upward and then came right back down. "Yes. I will make that happen."

"And did you find any fingerprints on the bat?"

"Yes."

She waited. "And? Do you know who they belong to?"

He looked down and smoothed out his pant legs. "You didn't hear it from me."

She nodded and leaned closer to him. "Of course not."

"They belonged to Richard Barney."

She gasped as the door clicked open behind her. She didn't need to turn around to see who it was. The clop clop of heavy clogs gave the female detective away.

"Thanks for coming in," Chip said. "Can you show yourself out?"

She nodded and got up quickly, avoiding Slaughter's eyes as she vacated the office. The burden of her guilty conscience had been lifted, but it had been replaced with a heavy, cold knowledge. Richard Barney was a killer.

Chapter 17

Only hours after Sandra left Chip's office, Ethel called to ask Sandra if she knew why the church was full of policemen. Sandra didn't want word getting out that she'd broken into the church and then told the police that some files were missing from the secretary's locked office, so she just said, "They're probably checking the security cameras." Ethel was shocked to learn that the church had security cameras. Sandra hurried to get off the phone and then wondered why she'd done so. What was she going to do now? It wasn't like she could go hang out at the church while Chip's team dusted the place.

But there was no denying that she was now in this thing. No more pretending to sit this one out. Angel helper or no angel helper, she was going to help Chip solve this thing, if not do it for him.

So, what was her next move? She couldn't learn more about the weapon. She *could* learn more about Richard, but she didn't think it would be a good idea to go knock on the door of his mansion and tip him off that the police were onto him. Best let them make that announcement. Where did that leave her? The motive. Why would Richard kill Phoenix? She had to learn more about the victim.

It took her a half hour to locate her laptop among piles and piles of books and toys. She flipped it open only to find that its battery was dead. Another half hour later, she found the charging cord. She plugged it in and plopped down to finally do her research when Sammy woke from his nap and started screaming. This made her feel like screaming. She'd finally decided to focus on this thing, and life wouldn't let her. She left the computer to charge and went to rescue Sammy from the Pack 'n Play. He was delighted to see her and made it clear he wanted to eat. *Now.* She propped him up in his high chair, poured some no-pulp orange juice into his sippy cup, and then dumped some Cheerios out in front of him. He kicked his chubby little legs in excitement as she slid her chair and laptop closer to him.

She typed Phoenix Haynes into the search bar and clicked enter. The results were not as helpful as she'd expected. They were all about something involving a Haynes in Phoenix, Arizona. She returned to the bar, put quotation marks around his name, and tried again.

The World Wide Web then told her that Phoenix Haynes was on Facebook. She clicked the link. *This* Phoenix had green hair and his lips pressed against an equally green lizard. Wrong Phoenix. She typed the name into the Facebook search bar, but there was only one Phoenix Haynes with a Facebook account. She returned to search the rest of the web and found a few more Phoenixes: a phys ed teacher in New Jersey; a rabbi in Seattle; and a marijuana activist in West Palm Beach. She didn't click, fairly sure that none of these were a match.

Maybe this wasn't going to work. A streak of electric blue flashed through her mind. *Hope House.* That's what Phoenix's T-shirt had said. It might not mean anything. He might have bought the shirt at Goodwill. Or maybe it meant a lot.

The new search returned 1.7 billion results in less than a second. She was just about to narrow it down when Nate came in from mowing the lawn. He glanced at the computer and then at her face. "Oh no. What are you doing?"

She decided to redirect. "Ethel called. The police are at the church."

He opened the fridge and bent to peer inside. "Good," he said into the box, "does that mean they don't think I did it?"

She laughed. "No. Chip doesn't suspect either of us." A Cheerio glanced off her cheek and onto the keyboard. She returned it to Sammy's tray.

Nate pulled the orange juice off the middle shelf and shut the door. Then he turned and leaned on the fridge. She cringed as she knew what he was going to do. He unscrewed the top of the jug and then tipped it back. He must have sensed her disdain because he paused his chugging long enough to lick his lips and say, "It's not gross if I finish it." Then he proceeded to polish it off. Good thing Sammy had gotten his serving when he did. Nate tossed the empty jug into the returnables bin and then wiped his lips again. "So, what are you looking up?"

"Who says I'm looking up anything? Maybe I'm just brushing up on my soccer rules."

He chortled. "Yeah, right. Like you don't know those rules by heart already."

This praise pleased her, but she still didn't want to tell him what she was doing.

"Does whatever you're doing have anything to do with the murder?"

"Maybe?" She tried to sound cute. She wasn't sure she pulled it off.

He rolled his eyes. "Just because Chip was nice to you this morning doesn't mean you can't get into trouble interfering."

"I know that."

He didn't look convinced. "Good. I'm going to go take a shower." He kissed Sammy on the top of his fuzzy head and then headed for the bedroom.

Sandra returned to her 1.7 billion options. The first result was a homeless shelter in New Mexico. The second was a homeless shelter in Atlanta. The third was a homeless shelter in White River Junction, Vermont. She sensed a pattern. She didn't think that a homeless shelter would have T-shirts, but she wasn't positive. She was about to start clicking on these shelter links when the fourth search result caught her eye—an addiction treatment center. Somehow, that seemed more like a T-shirt issuing institution. As soon as she clicked on the link, she knew. This was the place. The landing page was emblazoned with the same white logo that had been on the shirt. She didn't know if Phoenix had been a patient there, had known someone who was a patient there, or had worked there, but it was the best lead she'd had. And this Hope House was located in Lewiston—less than an hour away.

She looked at Sammy. She couldn't leave until Nate got out of the shower. And Joanna had practice in a few hours. Was Nate going to be willing to play chauffeur for a few hours? Would he be willing to *be her* for a few hours? She wasn't sure. She had to figure out a way to sweeten the pot.

She went into the bathroom. "Sweetie Pie?"

"Yeah?" The suspicion rang through the shower curtain.

"You remember that Japanese restaurant in Lewiston that you really like?"

"Yeah." The suspicion was growing.

"If you watch the kids for a few hours, I'll bring you back some scallop and shrimp hibachi."

He ripped the shower curtain back far enough so he could glare at her with one eyeball. "What's this about?"

"Exactly what I said. I need to run an errand in Lewiston—"

"You don't run errands in Lewiston! Tell me what this is really about before I run out of hot water."

She took a deep breath. "It's perfectly safe. Phoenix was wearing a Hope House T-shirt. Hope House is a rehab in Lewiston. I'm just going to go see if I can learn anything. And then I'll bring you seafood."

He narrowed his eyes. "Is Bob going with you?"

"I don't need Bob to run a simple errand! And no, he's not."

He shook his head. "I don't like it."

"Don't be ridiculous. I'll be fine. I will be safe." She waited for him to argue, but he didn't. "So, can you watch your children for a few hours? Joanna's got practice."

"Yep." He snapped the shower curtain shut. "But I don't want scallops. They'll be cold before you get home. I'll take filet mignon."

She wasn't sure why cold steak was preferable to cold seafood, but neither was she going to stand in the steamy bathroom and discuss it.

Chapter 18

Sandra hadn't even crossed the Plainfield town line when Bob appeared in the front seat beside her. This time, his materialization startled her less than it used to. She was becoming desensitized. "Hi." She tightened her grip on the steering wheel. "Come to talk me out of it?"

"No. I don't think I can. So I'm coming along to make sure you're safe."

Something about that didn't quite ring true. "You mean that you *want* to come along, right?"

At first he didn't answer her, but then he said, "Yeah, that too."

She sensed that Bob wasn't in the talking mood, so she waited as long as she could before saying, "Does this mean you're back?"

He looked sheepish. "For now, yes. But don't get used to it. I just think that this is valid. The police aren't paying attention to who the victim *was*. I think this is a good idea."

She gaped at him. "How do you know so much about what's going on? I thought you were staying out of it!"

He shrugged. "I hear things."

"Sure."

"I mean it. I haven't been snooping. I just hear things."

"So have you *heard* who Phoenix is?"

"No. It's a big secret. That's why I think this is a good idea." He reclined his seat with a bang. "Besides, I needed a nap, and the movement of this minivan always soothes me."

She laughed so hard that she feared she'd offended him, but when she glanced his way to see if he appeared irked, he appeared instead to be sound asleep.

It's just like driving my children around, she thought and turned up the radio.

Forty minutes later she had to turn the music down so she could better hear her GPS's directions to Hope House.

"You don't need the GPS. I know where it is."

Another world heard from. "Yes, but you were snoring."

"I wasn't snoring." He sat up straight and squared his shoulders. "Angels don't snore."

This was not true.

"It's right there." He pointed at a tall white house.

She estimated circa 1890 and shuddered to think how much it would cost to heat it. "Yes, I know. My GPS just told me that." She eased the van into the small parking lot and turned the engine off. Then she looked at the angel who felt very much like an old friend. "Are you ready?"

He gave her a small but incredibly reassuring smile. "By all means."

She led the way to the front door, knowing that to any onlookers, she appeared to be traveling alone. Despite the fact that her partner was invisible, his presence gave her as much reassurance as if he were visible to everyone. She took a deep breath and then reached for the doorknob. She turned and pushed and nothing.

"There's a buzzer," Bob said softly.

Duh. It was right there beside the door. She reached out and pushed the red button.

"How can I help you?" a pleasant, lilting voice came through the speaker.

She wasn't quite prepared for the difficulty of that question. She'd planned to just wing the conversation, but winging it was far easier in person, face to face. It was hard to wing it with a squawk box. "Uh ... it's hard to explain. I need to talk to someone about a friend of mine." Her voice came up on the end as though she were asking the box a question. If there hadn't been a tiny camera pointed at her face, she would've slapped herself in the forehead—Phoenix hadn't exactly been a friend.

After a hesitation, the box asked, "What is your name?"

She introduced herself, and the door gave a loud click. "Come on in."

She pulled the door open and stepped into a dimly lit hallway. As her eyes adjusted, she saw that a sliding glass window stood open, and a smiling woman stared at her expectantly. "Who's your friend?"

Great. The lie that just kept on giving. She stepped up to the window, wishing the sudden lump in her throat could have held off. "His name was Phoenix Haynes."

The woman's eyes widened with obvious recognition. "*Was?*"

She nodded. "I'm so sorry to be the bearer of bad news. I didn't know if you all knew." She looked around but there didn't seem to be a "you all." There was just this one woman, who now had tears in her eyes.

"What happened?"

Sandra shifted her weight from foot to foot, and the woman's eyes followed her as she rocked. What was she supposed to say to this? "Uh ... he was killed. Murdered, they think." Of course he was murdered. Why had she said, "they think"? The man hadn't accidentally fallen onto a bat. "Yeah, definitely murdered." She wanted to slap herself again, and she almost did this time.

A tear slid down the woman's rouged cheek. "What do you need from us?"

"I'm not sure," she admitted. "But I just ... I just want to learn more about Phoenix. I'm trying to figure out what happened to him—"

"You're not a cop." It was an observation, not a question.

"No."

"So then why aren't the cops here?"

Sandra opened her mouth, but no words came out. She started rocking again. Finally, she managed, "I don't know. But that's why I'm here. I'm not sure how hard they're working to figure this thing out, and I just ..."

"I'm sorry." The woman's eyes were dry now and her voice was taut. Something had changed. She was now suspicious of Sandra. "I can't tell you anything. We have privacy laws we abide by."

"I understand. And I'm not asking about anything medical, or even personal. I just hoped someone knew him and knew what he might have been doing in Plainfield."

"He was in Plainfield?" She was interested again.

"Yes. Isn't that weird?"

She didn't answer, but she didn't disagree. It *was* weird. No one went to Plainfield except college students, and most of those fled soon after their final semester. She didn't want to be judgy, but Phoenix hadn't looked like a college student.

"Well, I'm sorry, but I still can't tell you anything." She reached up to slide the glass window shut.

Sandra stuck her hand into the gap to stop her, and she reeled back as if Sandra had just grown aggressive. "Please," Sandra said, "do you know why he was in Plainfield?"

She shook her head and then, without turning her head, glanced up and to the right. Sandra followed her gaze and found that there was another tiny camera pointed at this woman's head. Sandra didn't know if she was trying to point the camera out or if she was just looking at it for her own purposes, but either way, Sandra was convinced to stop pushing. "Do you have any scrap paper?"

The woman frowned.

"Please?" Sandra rummaged through her purse for a pen, and by the time she found one, the woman had produced a small piece of paper. Sandra scribbled her number down and said, "Thanks for your time. I didn't mean to bother you. If you think of anything, I'd appreciate a call." She started to walk away and then said, "I just want to find out the truth. What happened to him, it was just so ..." She didn't know how to finish that sentence.

"Unfair," the woman finished for her. "It was so unfair. He worked so hard to come back to life, and now it's over."

Chapter 19

As Sandra slowly descended the front steps of Hope House, she heard "*Psst*" from behind her. She whirled around, but didn't see anyone there. She waited a moment, listening. "Hello?"

She looked at Bob for direction, but he just stared in the direction of the noise. She stood there for several seconds, until she began to believe she was imagining things. Giving up, she turned to head for the van again, and the hidden whisperer gave an encore performance.

Sandra changed direction and walked toward the noise. She came around the corner of the building and at first, thought there was no one there. Then she saw the face in the window. She started, having not expected to see a face pressed up against the screen.

"Why are you asking about Phoenix?" the girl asked.

Sandra tentatively stepped closer to the creepy image and the girl leaned back an inch, so the screen was no longer molded to the shape of her face. "Did you know him?"

She nodded. She had long, blond hair and round cheeks that looked extra-pink against her pale complexion. "I heard you talking. What happened?" Her voice trembled.

"I'm afraid that he was murdered. Someone assaulted him in the woods of Plainfield. I'm sorry you have to hear it like this." From a stranger. Through a window screen.

The girl stared at her without saying any more.

Sandra knew she should ask questions, but none were forthcoming.

"Ask her why he was in Plainfield," Bob said.

"Do you have any idea why he might have been in Plainfield?" She felt like an angel puppet. She didn't mind.

The girl didn't move. She might never have heard of Plainfield. Sandra took a step closer. Now *her* face was almost pressed against the screen. "I'm sorry, I should have introduced myself. I'm Sandra."

Still nothing.

"What's your name?" She tried to sound friendly, but it sounded insincere in their current setting.

"Tiara. You should go." Her voice was soft and squeaky. Tears were imminent.

Sandra stepped back. "Hi, Tiara. I'll go, I will, but I want to find out what happened to Phoenix. If you know anything that could help me, please tell me. Do you know if he had any enemies? Had he made anyone angry—"

"No!" she cried, sounding defensive. "Phoenix was a nice guy!"

"I'm sure he was, but lots of not-nice guys live on the streets, and if Phoenix was forced to deal with them, maybe he ran into some trouble?" The look on Tiara's face made Sandra stop talking.

"The streets? Phoenix wasn't homeless. He lived here. And he had a job."

"I'm sorry," Sandra said quickly. "I didn't mean to insult him—"

"You need to go." Her voice quavered. Was she scared of something?

"Are you in danger? If you are, I can get you help—"

"Go!" If it had been fear, it was now anger. Maybe it had never been fear.

Sandra nodded quickly. "Okay, okay." She reached into the bowels of her purse. She really needed to clean this thing out. Maybe even get a new one. Her fingers pushed past the lip balm, cough drops, hair elastics, and Burger King napkins and then closed around the pen. "Just let me give you my num—"

The window slammed shut.

"—ber," Sandra finished to no one. Tiara had vanished into the shadows of her room. Still, Sandra stood there until she found a receipt to write on, and then she wrote down her first name and phone number. She started to place it near the window, but then took it back to add, "I'm so sorry," on the bottom. Then she slid as much of it as she could between the window frame and the wall. She stood there for a few seconds to make sure it wouldn't fall out or blow away. Then she turned to go and Bob followed closely behind.

"She knows something," he said.

"Probably, but it's not necessarily pertinent. I feel so bad for her. It's bad enough battling through rehab, and then I tell her that her friend's been murdered. I hope I didn't just make her recovery harder for her."

"Wait." He put a hand on her arm and she stopped walking.

She looked up at him expectantly.

"I think I should go in."

Her surprise kept her wordless for several seconds. "Go in?"

He nodded, glancing at the front steps. "Yes. He's got to have a file in there, right? They won't know I'm there."

Use his supernatural invisibility to take a peek at Phoenix's file? It was brilliant! Why hadn't *she* thought of that? Because Bob was an angel, a well-behaved angel, who didn't do stuff like that. "Really?" She tried to measure her words. She wanted him to do it, but she didn't want him to get into trouble. "That's not an ethical violation?"

He stared at the front of the building as if the peeling paint held answers. "I don't think so. I'm not going to tell anyone anything that I see, and he's gone from this life now, so ..." Was he trying to convince her or himself? His eyes dropped to hers. "I think I need to do it. I want him to have justice."

She nodded. He wanted what she wanted. "The idea grows more enticing the longer you sit with it, doesn't it?"

He gave her a small smile. "More than enticing. I'm going in." And he was gone.

She looked around, wondering what to do with herself now. Should she drive away, let him catch up? He hadn't given her instructions. She didn't want to go sit in the hot van. People would wonder why she was staking out the place. She noticed a stone bench along a fence on the edge of the property. It didn't look comfy, but there was shade. She headed that way.

After she'd been sitting there for a few minutes, had checked the clock ten times and her Facebook feed twelve times, a man approached. "New here?"

She looked up at him and forced a smile. Though she wasn't doing anything wrong, she still felt guilty. "No, I'm not ..." How should she say this? She didn't want to insult the people who did live here. "I'm not staying. I was just trying to help a friend."

"Ah!" He sounded as if he understood completely. He sat down beside her, and she instinctively slid over to give herself a buffer. He didn't seem threatening, but the situation still felt too intimate. "And where's this friend?"

She sighed. How to answer that? "He's gone."

He looked around. "Gone? Like he took off?"

Something like that. "No, he's ... he died." Might as well go for the gold. "Maybe you knew him. His name was Phoenix Haynes?"

The man's jaw dropped open. "Phoenix is dead? When? How?" His cheeks grew pale.

She looked at the ground, feeling as though she should give him more privacy in his grief. "He was murdered. In Plainfield. Police don't know anything, that I know of."

After a long silence that was surprisingly comfortable, the man stuck out his hand. "Jake."

She accepted the handshake. "Nice to meet you, Jake. Wish it were under better circumstances."

He let go of her hand and patted her on the back. "Me too. And I'm sorry for your loss."

Her guilt returned. "I didn't actually know Phoenix. Still don't, really. I just ..." Why were words always so hard to locate and then put into a sensible order? "After he died, I just felt so bad. I wanted to help figure out who did it."

He blew out a puff of air and shifted in his seat. "Was he back to using?"

"I have no idea." Wait, she could do better than that. "I have no reason to think so." She looked at Jake. "Did you know him well?"

He shrugged. "'Bout as well as you can know anyone, I guess."

"Any idea who would be mad enough to kill him?"

He shook his head quickly. "No way. Phoenix wasn't a troublemaker. Unless he got mixed up in a deal gone bad, I can't think what could have happened."

She didn't think he'd gotten mixed up in a drug deal gone bad in the woods behind a church in Plainfield. "No enemies that you know of?"

"Nope. But we've all got skeletons in our closets." He stared at the side of the building, analyzing a different patch of that fascinating chipped white paint.

"Any idea of what connection Phoenix would have to Plainfield?"

He chuckled, but it sounded humorless. "Lady, I don't even know where Plainfield is." He paused. "And I don't know where Phoenix was from. Sorry."

Bob appeared in the middle of the lawn and waved her over. She gave Jake another smile. "Well, I'm going to go. But really, it was nice to meet you. Thanks for chatting with me."

He didn't look away from the white. "Yeah, you too. You might want to ask Tiara. She and Phoenix had a thing."

Sandra's eyes drifted to the still empty, still closed window, where her note fluttered in the breeze.

Chapter 20

Sandra climbed into the minivan and Bob teleported his way in. She noticed that he didn't buckle his seatbelt. Why would he? If she decided to hit a moose, he could just teleport out of harm's way. She hoped he would then call for an ambulance to care for his non-teleporting friends.

"Well, what did you find out?"

He glanced toward the stone bench where Jake still sat. "I could ask you the same thing."

She started the van and cranked the air conditioning, even though it only blew hot air at their faces. Bob reached down and turned the fan down.

"You first," she said.

"I read his file."

"Either you're a fast reader, or it was a short file."

"Both. As we might have assumed, Phoenix had an addiction. He stayed here for six weeks and stayed sober that whole time. There was nothing in his file about any problems. Seems as though he was a model patient. It wasn't a very exciting collection of paperwork."

"Did you at least find out where he was from?"

"Yes!" He sounded excited. "Lewiston. I even got a home address, though I'm not sure what good it will do us."

"Tiara said he still lived at Hope House. Maybe that's his parents' place?"

"No idea, but I don't think we should bother his parents unless we think of a very good reason. I'm sure the police have already talked to them."

Sandra made no such assumption.

"Your turn. What did your new friend tell you?"

She was excited to think she might have learned more than he had, without the benefit of invisibility. "He said Phoenix wasn't a troublemaker and didn't have any enemies." She paused and wished she knew how to do a steering wheel drum roll. "And he said that Phoenix and Tiara had a thing."

"A thing?"

"Yes."

"What is a thing?"

Was he joking? He was an angel, not an imbecile. "You know, like a relationship."

"Oh, that sort of thing." He paused, and she sensed his wheels were turning. "I had a feeling that might be the case, but as an angel, the nuances of romantic entanglements are often lost on me."

She had no idea what he'd just said.

"If I were a betting angel, I would bet that she calls you."

An influx of hope surged into Sandra's chest. "I certainly hope so." She started the car. "Even if she doesn't know anything, I'd love to talk to her again. I'm not even sure why, but I liked her."

"Yeah." Bob sounded contemplative. "I liked her too."

SANDRA CAME HOME TO chaos. Joanna and Nate had cooked, and they'd used every dish in the house to create something that loosely resembled lasagna. Meanwhile, Peter had sprinkled catnip on the living room carpet, and Mr. T had gone to town, shredding a square foot of the carpet in the exact middle of the living room. It would be a while before *that* would get replaced—Sandra could almost hear the cash register dinging in response.

At least Sammy looked safe and sound. She scooped him out of the Pack 'n Play to see he'd left a large brown patch behind. She looked down at his onesie and saw the blowout. "Nate!" she called, trying not to sound too irate. "When was the last time you changed Sammy?"

Peter looked sheepish. "I did it like twenty minutes ago. Why, did I do it wrong?"

"No, of course not. Will you please get Mr. T away from the living room and then vacuum? I'm going to go give Sammy a bath."

"Okay." He sounded hesitant.

She kept walking.

"You want me to vacuum Mr. T? Why don't we just buy a Cat Vac?"

"No!" she called back without slowing down. She was suddenly in a great hurry to get the bathroom door shut behind her. "Vacuum up the catnip!" She didn't even know if there was any catnip left, but if there was, she wanted it in the vacuum, not in the carpet. And no way was she going to buy a Cat Vac. First of all, they cost a zillion dollars, and second, her baser self did not want to add to the Barney fortune. The Cat Vac was what had turned Richard Barney into an empire. Before he'd invented the odd contraption, he'd just been an ordinary veterinarian. But then he'd invented the small box into which people shoved their cats to have them "shed in six seconds" and the money had started falling from the sky. She rolled her eyes at the thought and slammed the bathroom door.

Chapter 21

Nary a Bickford showed up for the next softball practice. Sandra wasn't surprised. It was Saturday night, and she thought probably the Bickfords had more "social" things to do. She casually mentioned this to her husband, who was quick to jump to the Bickfords' defense and correct her. Adam had let him know well in advance that they were all playing in a men's league tournament that weekend.

She set the brakes on Sammy's stroller and sat down on the dugout bench beside her husband. "Oh yeah, Danny mentioned that they all played in a men's league. I didn't know there was such a thing."

He raised an eyebrow. "Danny? You're on a first name basis with the Bickfords now?"

"Yes. I am, after all, their scorekeeper."

He snickered. "So, anyway, yes, there is such a thing. Local businesses sponsor teams and they pay to play in big tournaments in Auburn and Portland. The winners get actual money."

She was incredulous. "Seriously?"

"Those involved take it pretty seriously, but I had no idea that Adam and his family were involved when I invited him to play." He chuckled. "Turns out my invitation made far more sense than I thought at the time."

"Yes, it sure did. He was probably flattered. So, they're not *skipping* practice. They're just with one of their other teams tonight. That means they're coming back, right?" Nate studied her face, and too late, she realized she'd sounded overly excited about that idea. She shrugged. "Sorry, I kind of like them."

Nate nodded. "I like them too. They are entertaining. But for now, I guess we just practice with what we've got." He spoke with the same tone he would use to declare, "Now it's time to clean the bathroom." At least, she imagined that's how he would sound if he ever declared he was going to clean a bathroom. She'd never heard such a declaration, and doubted she ever would.

Nate walked out onto the field, where Pastor Cliff was announcing batting practice. Both Barneys were in attendance, making Sandra wonder why they hadn't arrested Richard yet, if his prints were on the weapon. Then she wondered if Chip and gang had found any prints in the secretary's office—any prints other than her own.

Daphne Barney sat in the bleachers with her girls surrounding her. They were all holding still for once—they were probably too hot to run around—and Sandra was able to count them. There appeared to be only four. No way. She could've sworn there were more of them. Maybe one was at a friend's house. But did the Barney girls even have friends? She'd never seen them playing with other children, despite her church having a gazillion children in regular attendance. It struck her then that she barely knew these people, even though they'd been going to her church for a while now. She felt a little guilty, so she headed for the bleachers.

As she sat, she asked, "Hot enough for you?" It was a line so commonly delivered in Maine whenever the temperature went above seventy-five, she hoped it would serve as a harmless segue into a friendly conversation.

She was wrong.

"I'm from South Carolina." Daphne's face was so tight Sandra wondered if she'd just had a Botox shot. Her tone was so unfriendly, Sandra almost bounced right off the bleacher seat and ran away.

"Sorry, didn't mean to insult your ability to tolerate heat." She hoped her words didn't sound as sarcastic as she'd felt when she spoke them.

Daphne's face exploded into a beauty pageant smile. "No, I'm sorry. I truly am. I guess I'm just grumpy." She leaned closer and whispered, "I hate softball."

Sandra laughed. "Yeah, it's not my favorite either."

Daphne rocked away from her. "Yes, I've heard you're quite the soccer hero around here." Her words teetered on the edge of ironic, and Sandra wasn't sure whether to be offended, so she gave her the benefit of the doubt.

"Mommy, will you please braid my hair?" One of the blondes plopped down on the bleacher in front of her, and as if on autopilot, Daphne's hands began weaving the long locks together. Sandra noticed then how perfect Daphne's hair was. And she wasn't sweating, which didn't seem reasonable. Maybe this was a benefit of growing up in South Carolina—you learned not to sweat.

"So, four girls, huh?" She cringed at her awkwardness, but she couldn't stand the suspense of not knowing exactly how many children Brendan and Daphne had.

"Yes. This is Brenna." She pointed with her chin without looking away from her braiding. "That is my oldest, Bethany. And then down there we have Bonnie and Beatrice. Get out of the dirt, girls!" The girls popped up like those old bounce back punching bags her dad had blown up for her when she was little, back when it was okay to teach kids to punch. In perfect synchrony, Bonnie and Beatrice plopped down on the front row of the bleachers and stared out at the batting practice, which could not possibly have interested them. It didn't even appear to be interesting the people directly involved in it. "Who knows what's in that dirt," Daphne said, mostly to herself.

Sandra considered the question, but decided it was probably mostly dirt in that dirt.

Richard Barney stepped up to bat and missed the first pitch. Then he missed the second. And the third. Sandra wasn't sure if he was a terrible batter or if Pastor Cliff was a terrible pitcher. She watched another five missed swings and decided that both things were true.

A large sedan pulled into the church parking lot, and it took Sandra too long to realize it was Chip and Slaughter. They climbed out and walked out onto the field as if they owned the place. They made a beeline for Richard, said something to him, and then in a move that nearly knocked the wind out of Sandra's lungs, spun him around and slapped some handcuffs on his wrists.

At that, his church brethren made a mad dash to surround him. Sandra didn't know if they were there to defend him or if they just wanted to get closer to the drama. All she knew was that she wished *she* were closer to the drama. She did stand and climb out of the bleachers, only then realizing that the Barneys beside her seemed awfully calm about the whole thing. Or maybe they didn't understand what was going on? She pulled her eyes away from the action to glance at Daphne, whose face was completely impassive. Were South Carolinians stoics? Was Daphne related to Slaughter? They should form a poker team.

She turned back to what appeared to be an arrest and tried to read Chip's lips. Pastor Cliff seemed to be enthusiastically defending Richard Barney's honor. Sandra wasn't surprised. He didn't want to lose the biggest tither he'd ever had to the clink.

Sandra realized then that she didn't think Richard had done it either, no matter what the fingerprints suggested. Why would a rich man kill a peaceable recovering drug addict? And why would he do it with an old softball bat? Didn't rich people hire real criminals to carry out their crimes? At least, that's how it happened on television. Then it had to be a crime of passion, right? Something Richard hadn't thought out in advance? But how could Richard have any passion regarding Phoenix?

This whole business had started out with a bunch of puzzle pieces that didn't seem to fit together, and she feared Chip and Slaughter were trying to jam the pieces into the wrong spots.

Chapter 22

Sandra took her coffee outside. The Sunday morning mayhem of her house was getting to her more than it usually did, and she needed a minute to collect her thoughts. She had spent most of the night tossing and turning, worried that Chip and Slaughter had arrested the wrong man. She wasn't the president of the Richard Barney fan club, but neither did she think that he was a murderer. She drained the last drop of her creamy java and was reluctantly returning to the circus tent when she noticed a man standing a few feet from her bird bath.

It was Bob. He wasn't looking at her, but was staring at a bird with such intensity Sandra wondered if he was reading its thoughts. She approached slowly, trying to be quiet, even though it didn't require much effort; her slippers sliding through dewy grass didn't make much noise.

"Good morning," he said.

Angel ears at their finest.

"Good morning. Sorry, I didn't mean to interrupt."

He finally looked at her. "Interrupt what?"

She pointed her chin at the chickadee. "Whatever interaction you're having with your fellow winged creature." She figured this was as good a time as any. "*Do* you have wings, Bob?"

Before she could finish the question, he returned his gaze to the bird. "We weren't chatting. I was just admiring her feathers."

She waited for him to answer her question. "So, is the other thing proprietary?" She grinned, trying to cover up how much she really wanted to know whether he had wings and if so, where were they?

"They arrested Richard Barney."

83

"Yes, I know." She was never going to know, this side of heaven anyway, if Bob could fly.

"And you don't think they've got the right man?"

She paused. "How do you know that?"

He shrugged, still staring at the chickadee.

She stepped closer, and of course, the bird took off, but Bob continued to stare at the small waves traveling through the water, the only evidence that the bird had ever been there.

"I can see it on your face. You are distraught about something. So, either you're worried about being late for church"—he glanced at her and looked her up and down—"and I doubt that's the case given your outfit, or you're thinking about the case. And you don't look relieved that the murderer has been caught. You are unsettled. So, if not Richard Barney, then who? Who did it?"

She pulled her worn bathrobe tighter around her, feeling self-conscious. "I have no idea. It could be him. I don't think he's a particularly nice man, although his son seems far crueler." She took a deep breath, really wishing her coffee mug wasn't empty. Was it too much to ask Bob to miraculously refill it? And with that Cumberland Farms coffee from down the street? She could go back inside and fill in with non-miraculous Folgers, but Bob had a habit of disappearing if she didn't keep him completely engaged. She decided to go without. "But it's not that I think he's innocent so much as that I think their version of the crime doesn't make sense."

He turned toward her and gave her a broad smile. "You're really starting to sound like a detective."

"Speaking of detectives, can't you just go eavesdrop on Chip and Slaughter? Maybe they know stuff we don't know?"

He chuckled. "First of all, do you know how weird it is that you call him by his first name and her by her last? And second, I've told you before that I can't just go eavesdropping. There are rules, guidelines ..." He acted as if he wanted to say more.

She wished he would. This whole angel thing was so mysterious. She'd spent all this time with him and she hardly knew any more than when she first met him in the grocery store parking lot. He never added to his sentence, and the pause grew long and uncomfortable.

"I feel like I know Chip, even though I really don't, and so I think of him on a first name basis. As for Slaughter, well, her last name just sort of fits her." As she discussed the topic aloud, it further developed in her mind. "And they're sort of like a unit. So they get a first name and a last. Collectively, they are Chip Slaughter."

He laughed again. "That doesn't make any sense, but if it works for you ... so, what do you think Chip Slaughter has wrong?"

She hesitated, wanting to sound smart. "All of it. First of all, Richard Barney is loaded, thanks to his cat vacuum thing—"

Bob's face jerked back in alarm. "Cat vacuum? Someone is vacuuming up cats?"

She laughed and shook her head quickly, wanting to comfort him. A new chickadee landed in the bath. Or maybe it was the same one. But this one looked chubbier. Bob returned part of his attention to the bird bath. "No, silly." She stepped closer, and the new bird flew off. She was happy to see it go, finding herself a tad jealous of Bob's attention. "It's a small box that you put your cat in, and it sucks out all the extra hair, so they don't shed all over your house."

The alarm returned to Bob's face. "That's barbaric!"

She laughed again, this time with her belly, and slapped a hand over her mouth to try to keep the noise down. She didn't need her neighbors wondering why she was laughing hysterically at an empty bird bath. "It doesn't hurt them. It's supposed to be gentle." She shrugged and turned her own gaze to the empty bird bath. Now that she had his full attention, it was too much to handle. "Anyway, so he's loaded. Why would he need to kill a recovering drug addict from Lewiston? And if he did, would he really be stupid enough to do it in his church's backyard? I don't like the man, but I doubt the inventor of the Cat

Vac is stupid. But let's say that he is, that he's not smart enough to hire someone else to kill the man—"

"It might not be a matter of intelligence. The more people one involves in a crime, the more chance there is of being caught."

This insight surprised her. "You're sounding more like a detective too. What? You think he did it?"

He shrugged. "I don't know."

She rocked on her feet. She was getting tired of standing, and she needed more coffee.

"Continue." He twirled an impatient finger at her.

It took her a second to remember where she was. "Oh yeah, and so, let's say he did do it. You really think he'd be stupid enough to *return the bloody murder weapon to the bat bag?*"

Bob blinked. "You're right. That part doesn't make any sense. Why not just wipe the prints off it and leave it with the body? Then the whole softball team is under suspicion."

"Right! And he wasn't smart enough to wipe his prints off? Seriously? What criminal doesn't know enough not to wipe their prints off the murder weapon? Don't people watch television?"

Bob snorted. "I think people watch more than enough television. I would say that a person who was drinking, or using drugs, or overwhelmed by emotion or panic—*those* people don't remember the finer points of police procedural dramas."

"What?" She hadn't meant to snap, but he wasn't making any sense.

"Those people don't stop to think about how things work on television. Those people make bad decisions."

"Are you saying Richard was drunk or high or emotionally overwhelmed?"

"Maybe." Bob dragged the word out as if he wasn't sure he wanted to say it.

She couldn't picture Richard being any of these things. "Still. I think it sounds more like a frame job. Like someone *else* put the weapon back, to make sure that we found it. Of course, I have no idea how they got Richard's prints on the bat. I didn't think he would stoop low enough to touch the old thing."

"I know how his prints got on the bat," a small voice spoke from behind them.

Sandra almost shrieked in surprise. "Peter! What are you doing sneaking up on us?" She put her arm around his shoulders and pulled him closer, already wondering how annoyed he'd be if she asked him to go get her more coffee.

"I didn't sneak. You were just talking a lot." He looked around, raising his voice a little as he said, "And since I know you don't talk to birds, I figured Bob was here ... somewhere."

She shushed him and pointed to her right.

Peter's eyes widened, and she knew that he could now see Bob.

"Hi, Peter."

"Bob!" Peter stepped out from under Sandra's arm and flung his spindly limbs around Bob's waist with such force that Bob staggered back a step.

"Peter!" she whispered. "The neighbors!"

Peter made it clear he didn't care what the neighbors saw or thought. He stepped back still beaming.

"So?" she cried. "How did his prints get on the bat?"

Peter rolled his shoulders back and raised his chin. "At the game before the murder, Mr. Barney, the younger, was making fun of the team bats. He handed a bat to the old Mr. Barney, and said, 'Just try to swing it! It weighs a ton!' They both swung a couple of the bats, laughing and being mean."

"Then what?" she pushed.

He scrunched his face up. "Then nothing, I guess. I don't know. I wasn't really paying attention."

Bob ruffled Peter's hair. "Good job, buddy." He looked at Sandra. "Sounds like maybe Brendan is the framer."

Her breath caught. "And Richard is the framed."

A male chickadee landed on the edge of the bath and sang out *fee-bee!* like an eerie endorsement of their new theory.

They all stood there silently staring at the bird, but it went mute.

"You should go get more coffee and then get to church."

She frowned. "How do you know I need more coffee?"

"You keep staring at the empty cup in your hand."

She glanced down at it again. "If you can read people so well, why can't you pick out killers?"

"I probably could if I knew whom to look at it and spent enough time at it." He jumped a little. "So, that's what we're going to do! If Brendan is in church, study his every move. I'll go too and do the same."

"Won't that get you into trouble with Mannaziah?" She was sure she'd pronounced that wrong.

He shrugged. "We'll find out." And he was gone.

Chapter 23

Sandra left Sunday school early to snag a good seat in the sanctuary for the main service. And while she knew it was for a good cause, she was still worried about upsetting the apple cart. She knew she couldn't just *change seats*. Changing seats meant stealing someone else's seat. In some cases, it meant stealing a seat from someone who'd sat in that spot for forty years. People were mostly tolerant of this behavior from guests, but she wasn't a guest. She took the very front seat on the far left side of the room, miles away from where she and her family usually sat. She knew people would notice. She hoped Brendan Barney wouldn't. And she didn't think he would. She thought he'd have more pressing issues on his mind.

She didn't know whose spot this normally was, and hoped that maybe it was unclaimed, though it wasn't likely. It truly was a terrible seat, which was why she'd chosen it. If one sat in this spot, and faced front, all they could see was the door to the plastic flowers closet and the corner of the altar. Hence, anyone normal sitting here would *have* to sit sideways in order to see the pastor. She tried this sideways position now, and was thrilled at how well it worked. She could see the entire sanctuary, but she didn't even need to. Unless Brendan Barney also got creative with his choice of seats, she'd easily be able to discreetly stare at him for the entire service.

A thought flickered through her mind, sending her heart into a panic. What if he didn't come to church? His father was in jail! Maybe he'd want the day off. Or maybe he'd be too ashamed to come. But the Barneys were all about keeping up appearances. They were practically Stepfords. So they'd come, right? Unless they decided that it would look better if they *didn't* come. Maybe they'd stay home to give the appearance of grieving, or of solidarity with their patriarch. She shook her head. She was giving herself a headache. She texted her husband, "I've changed seats for today. We're up front. Please don't make a big deal. I'll explain later." She hoped he'd forget to ask for this promised explanation, because he wasn't going to like it.

Sunday school hadn't been dismissed yet, but those churchgoers who didn't attend Sunday school started trickling in. And they sure were a lively, talkative bunch. Sandra hadn't realized this, as she was always still in class. She stared down at her phone, scrolling through her Facebook feed without actually seeing anything, trying to be small and unnoticeable.

Her efforts failed. The sanctuary was half-full when a small, tan boy with a mass of curly blond hair that nearly doubled his height appeared in front of her with wide eyes. "Hey! That's *our* seat!" Sandra could feel the room full of eyeballs burning into the back of her head. She wasn't sure how to respond to the child, so she just stared at him, wishing the moment would be over. "Move!" he cried, pointing to the entire sanctuary behind her. Good thing she was in the front row with only this semi-feral child looking at her, because her cheeks were on fire.

"Gabriel!" a woman snapped from the aisle.

Oh thank heavens, the cavalry has arrived.

The woman who was probably Gabriel's mother grabbed his hand and yanked him toward the wall and then into the row behind Sandra. "I'm so sorry," she said as she maneuvered him into his new seat.

Sandra didn't dare speak. She didn't want to call any more attention to herself than she already had.

"But she's in my spot!" the child whined, not sounding so fierce anymore.

"She can sit wherever she wants," the mom said, and Sandra wished she knew the woman's name, but she *was* from the other side of the church. Whoever she was, it didn't sound as though she believed what she was saying.

"But this is where Elisha's family sits!" His whining made Sandra long for nails on a chalkboard.

Her husband appeared then, looking bewildered. She gave her head a slight shake, trying to telepathically beg him not to mention their new locale. But the telepathy failed when it reached Joanna, who cried out at the top of her voice, "Why are we sitting up front, Mommy?" Sandra wanted to die, right then and there. It would be so convenient. They'd all already be dressed and ready for the funeral.

"Sit down, honey." Sandra's voice was hardly audible.

Joanna opened her mouth, but Peter snapped, "Be quiet, Joanna!"

Not normally scolded by her big brother, Joanna's mouth snapped shut. Sandra gave Peter a grateful look and resisted the urge to turn around and see how many people were still staring at them—the front row squatters. Instead, she continued to stare at the door of the plastic flowers closet until the service started. In fact, she didn't move until she stood for the music and though the rest of the congregation stood with her, she still felt conspicuous.

By the end of the music, she had calmed down—the power of melody, maybe—and as the pastor stepped behind the pulpit, she finally turned sideways in her seat so that she could see him. Her peripheral vision informed her that the sanctuary was packed. It was usually fairly full, except for fourth of July weekend, but this was nuts. Had the arrest attracted visitors? Had people come just to lay eyes on the family of the accused? Were people that morbid?

Sandra scanned the large room to see if the Barneys were even there, and immediately made eye contact with Daphne Barney. And it wasn't a pleasant eye contact. It was a laser shot out of Daphne's eyes that suggested that Daphne knew they'd changed seats, knew why they'd changed seats, and had been staring at her for eons, trying to set her on fire with her vision.

Not daring to look to either side of Daphne to see if Brendan was present, Sandra returned her eyes to Pastor Cliff, who looked beyond grieved. She realized he'd been talking about Richard and tuned in.

"... be mindful that the police have a difficult job. I don't mean to be critical of their efforts. I know they are doing the best that they can. But I also know Richard Barney"—

Unless he knew Richard before they'd moved to town, he hadn't known him for long.

—"and I can tell you that he is not a murderer. So please join me as we pray that this can all be resolved soon and Richard can be returned to his family." He bowed his head and squeezed his eyes shut.

"Can we also pray for the victim's family?" Elder Vern called out.

"Of course," Cliff muttered without looking up. As he began to pray, Sandra's mind wandered, first to the fact that, as far as she knew, Phoenix didn't have any family, and then, to the fact that this was the ideal time to scan the congregation and see what she could see. She opened her eyes and swung them toward the Barney row, where they again met Daphne's razor sharp gaze. She looked down quickly, her skin covered in gooseflesh; she was so frustrated with herself for still not knowing whether Brendan was there. Did Daphne always glare at her during prayer? She wouldn't know—they usually sat on the same side.

"What's wrong?" Nate whispered.

She realized that the prayer was over and she was still staring down at her knees, scowling. "Nothing," she whispered back. And that *should* be true. Why was she letting Daphne get to her so much? Of course the woman was upset. She probably felt as though everyone in the room was staring at her.

Sandra hazarded another look, and yep, Daphne caught her again, but this time, Sandra pretended not to notice. Instead, she verified that Brendan was in fact right there alongside his wife. He had his arms folded across his chest and his chin held high. He had bags under his eyes, but other than that, he looked the same as he always looked: arrogant. He didn't look guilty, which left her to wonder, *Do psychopaths feel guilt? Isn't that what makes them psychopaths?* Four little blond Barneys sat lined up on the other side of him. All present and accounted for—except for Richard Barney. She wondered what had happened to Mrs. Richard Barney. Was he widowed? Divorced? Maybe his ex-wife hated him enough to frame him.

Pastor Cliff cleared his throat, a noise that, when amplified through the house speakers, sounded like a donkey dying. It certainly got her attention. "I know this is an uncomfortable topic under the circumstances, but our church softball team *will* continue, and so, the elders and I have decided to set a few ground rules."

Oh, this should be rich. Were they going to make a no-murdering rule?

"First, there is absolutely no drinking or tobacco on church property, and church property includes the softball field. If anyone is seen drinking or using tobacco, they will not be allowed to play. Next, from now on, people are only allowed to play in games if they come to all the practices. And lastly, if they want to play in the games, they need to be here in church on the Sunday morning before the game."

Nate gave her a wide-eyed look, and she didn't bother to whisper when she said, "He can't be serious."

SANDRA MET BOB BACK at the bird bath. They had to be more discreet this time as it was later in the day, and there was a greater chance of witnesses. If she was going to continue having cloak-and-dagger meetings with angels in her backyard, she was going to have to put up a fence.

"Did you study him?" Bob asked studiously.

Sandra snickered. "I tried. I didn't learn anything." This wasn't exactly true. "Well, I guess I learned that Daphne is really mean. Or she hates me. Or both."

"Yes, I saw her glaring at you. She did not glare at me."

Sandra looked at him. She didn't know if he was trying to be funny. "So, what did you learn?"

"I tried. I really did. But it was difficult to read him. He seemed to not be experiencing any emotions, but instead, to be waiting for church to be over."

This made sense. "So our mission was a bust? I disrupted half the church's seating plan for nothing?"

Bob smirked. "Not for nothing. A young woman named Karissa was very happy that a young man named Steve was forced into her row."

Sandra didn't recognize either of these names and vowed to do a better job of knowing her fellow parishioners.

"Also, we learned that none of the Barneys are terribly upset about Richard's arrest. Or if they are, they are hiding it. But why would they bother to hide their sadness? I don't think they're very sad about it."

"I don't either," Sandra mumbled. "And that's pretty sad in itself."

Chapter 24

After suffering her second almost sleepless night in a row, Sandra determined that she needed to go talk to Chip. She didn't, however, want anything to do with Chip's other half, so she called him and asked if she could meet him for coffee. She stressed that she needed to talk to him alone, hoping he would infer that she couldn't handle a Monday morning dose of Slaughter.

Chip agreed and soon Sandra was sitting near a window at Aroma Joe's. Sammy was in a high chair beside her, working on his second donut hole, and the chair across from her was empty.

Chip was late.

She polished off her coffee and got up to get a refill, keeping one eye on her sugared-up son. As she paid the friendly barista, the bell over the door announced a new arrival, and Sandra spun to make sure it was Chip and not a softball-bat-wielding Barney.

It was Chip. She gave him a curt nod and returned to her seat. He followed.

She looked at his empty hands. "Don't you want a coffee?"

"I don't have much time. What do you need?"

She noticed then that he looked as exhausted as she felt. Pangs of sympathy ran through her chest. Sure, she enjoyed dabbling in the occasional mystery, but how stressful it must be to do this sort of thing day in and day out.

"I don't really need anything, but ... well ..." This had gone so much smoother when she'd rehearsed it in her head at 3 a.m.

He quirked an eyebrow.

Sammy screeched and flung some crumbs at him.

To his credit, he simply brushed off his sport coat and gave Sammy a sincere smile. "Yeah, I don't really like plain donuts either, bud." He looked at Sandra. "You should tell your mom to get you chocolate."

"Okay, so I think you've got the wrong guy," she spat out.

He sighed and leaned back in his chair, leaving one hand on the table. The other one dangled at his side as if it were too tired to do anything else. He didn't look surprised at her outburst. Quite the opposite, in fact. "And what makes you say that?"

She looked around the room and leaned closer to him. "What kind of an idiot puts a murder weapon back into a bat bag with his fingerprints and the victim's blood all over it?"

Again, no surprise on Chip's face. This line of reasoning had already occurred to him.

She sat up straight. "My son saw Brendan Barney get Richard to handle the bat. He put it right into his hands. Maybe he's trying to frame his father."

Without turning his head, he glanced at Sammy. "This son?"

"No, my old—"

He held up the hand that rested on the table. "I know, I know, I'm just joshing you. But, unfortunately, frame jobs are a TV thing. They rarely happen in real life."

That you know of, she thought. "And why is that unfortunate?"

"Because that would be an easy answer."

"Answer to what?"

"To our current problem." He returned his dangling arm to the table and folded his hands together. "I agree with you. I think we've got the wrong man."

What? "Then release him!"

He looked out the window. "I can't. It's not that simple. It doesn't matter what I *think*. What matters is what the evidence says."

They were quiet for a minute, and Sammy started humming a tune she was pretty sure was a Sammy original. "Then we need to find more evidence."

He returned his eyes to her. "Not *we*. The police will find the evidence. I appreciate all you've done to help the cause of justice in the last year, but don't get carried away." He glanced at Sammy. "Think of your kids. They don't want you getting hurt."

"Of course not!" She felt a little guilty. "I am *always* thinking of my kids."

He nodded. "Good." He started to get up.

"Do you want a statement from Peter?"

He straightened all the way up and looked down at her. "If we start looking at Brendan as a suspect, maybe."

"You're not looking at him as a suspect yet?"

He glared at her and shushed her, even though they were the only ones in the room. "I'm leaving now. Have a good day."

"Wait!" She grabbed his sleeve and stood up too. "What about the prints? Did you find anything in the secretary's office?"

He groaned. "We found *thousands* of prints in the secretary's office. We're still matching them, but so far, nothing suspicious."

"You mean no Richard or Brendan prints?"

He didn't gratify this with an answer, and she knew he was about to walk away.

"What happened to Richard's wife?"

His eyes narrowed. "Why?"

"Just wondering."

"Nothing happened to her that we know of. Sandra, if you know something, you need to tell us!"

She held her hands up. "I don't know anything! I just wanted to know if she was still alive."

Chip was no longer amused. "Yes, she's alive. They're divorced, and she lives in New Mexico. And you're *not* going to talk to her."

Yeah, right, like she was going to go to New Mexico. She shook her head and tried to think of something else to ask, while she had him right in front of her. "What's the relationship between Phoenix and Richard? I mean, what's the motive?"

"Sandra, I have to go. And you need a new hobby. Try mystery novels. Slaughter loves them."

Properly put in her place, she plopped down into her hard plastic chair. How dare he? She already read mystery novels! That didn't mean she couldn't be of help to him in real life. He obviously needed it, if he was keeping a man in jail when he knew he was innocent.

And Slaughter read mystery novels? Seriously? She'd always figured Slaughter spent her free time boxing a bag in her basement, going to the gun range, or hunting wild coyotes. She couldn't picture her curled up with a book.

The bell dinged as he left the building. "Let me know about the prints!" she called after him, but she didn't think he heard her. And even if he did, she didn't think he'd let her know about anything.

Chapter 25

Tuesday was game day, and for the first time in history, Sandra was looking forward to a church softball game. In fact, she kept checking the clock. At around one, Peter asked, "If Pastor said the Bickfords can't play, maybe I could play in this game?"

"Maybe," she said, without really thinking about it. Church softball was turning into a fairly dangerous game; did she even want her son involved? "You can ask Dad." Maybe she needed some help. She hadn't heard from Bob since their second backyard meeting on Sunday, and didn't know if he'd go to the softball game. She doubted it. He probably had a middle school sports commitment. She called Ethel. "Hey, want to come to the church softball game tonight?"

"I appreciate the invitation, but that's not really my cup of tea."

Sandra laughed at her honesty.

"Do you need me there for some reason?"

"No pressure, at all. It's just ... I've been trying to help the police with this whole thing—"

"You didn't really need to tell me that."

Sandra laughed again. "Right, of course. Well, if something happens tonight, and I end up, I don't know, chasing a bad guy into the woods"—she looked down at her flip-flops and vowed to wear proper sneakers just in case—"it would be great to know that someone was there with my kids."

There was a pause. "Are you *planning* to chase a bad guy into the woods?"

"No!" Sandra said quickly.

"Because when there's a plan, I like to know the plan."

"Of course! I would definitely tell you the plan if there was one, and I will if there is one. I just ... haven't heard from Bob lately, and I don't know if he'll be there—"

"Bob? What do you mean? Is he helping you with this? I didn't know he was back!"

"Well, he never actually *went* anywhere. He just became invisible. Anyway, he's sort of helping, but he hasn't done much, yet. Then again, neither have I. I don't know, Ethel. There hasn't been any action yet. That's why you haven't heard anything. But my gut tells me that there might be some action tonight."

"Your gut."

Sandra didn't know if she was asking for clarification. "Yes, my gut."

"All right then. I'll be there, with my bug spray. Do you have any extra lawn chairs? I am far too old for bleachers."

"Of course. Thank you, Ethel. You're the best."

SANDRA FORGOT ETHEL'S lawn chair. Her guilt nearly overwhelmed her, but Ethel was gracious.

"You can sit in here with me!" She motioned toward the metal bench in the dugout. "It's not much, but—"

"But it will keep me from getting hit by balls!" She scuttled inside.

"Not if the balls come from above."

Ethel glanced up at the open sky, and her face fell in disappointment. Then she sat down and started making funny faces at Sammy, who squealed in delight. "I guess you'll just have to save me from those!"

Peter appeared in front of the dugout. "You playing, Ethel?" He laughed at his own joke.

"I was thinking about it!"

"They might need you. There's no one here."

Sandra looked around the field and saw that Peter was only exaggerating a little. The field was littered with orange T-shirts from Faith Community folks from Rumford, but there was precious little representation for the home team. The Pastor was there, of course, as were Nate, Boomer, Loriana, and Lewis. But no Barneys or Bickfords. It was going to be hard to field a team with five people. She looked at her phone and saw that they still had ten minutes till game time. She left her children with Ethel and headed out onto the field, where Nate was playing catch with Boomer.

"Have you talked to Adam?"

Nate caught the ball and looked at her. "Not lately, why?"

"I mean, is he still planning to come?"

Nate held the ball and stared at her. "What do you mean?"

She stretched her arms out wide. "I mean, there's no one here. Maybe they'll still let him play."

He leaned closer to her. "I never told him he *couldn't* play." He stood back again and threw the ball to Boomer. "But I don't know if he's coming or not. Maybe his cousins decided this team isn't much fun." He gave her a sardonic look. "I wouldn't blame him."

The sound of an engine with no muffler filled the air, and she thought her heart might burst with joy. She winked at Nate and then trotted off, praying that Pastor Cliff wouldn't enforce his ridiculous new rules, at least not without giving the men fair warning.

They hadn't even all climbed out of the truck yet when Cliff approached them. She couldn't hear what he said, but she could see the incredulity on the men's faces. A small cluster of Bickfords formed around the sole non-Bickford and Sandra was thinking about interfering when she saw Nate headed that way. She sneaked closer just so she could listen in better. She didn't share her favorite angel's qualms about eavesdropping.

Her diplomatic husband said, "Pastor, I respect your guidelines, but I have to respectfully disagree with enforcing them here and now.

These men didn't know they were supposed to be at church or at practice."

She couldn't hear Cliff's response, and she crept closer.

One of the Bickfords turned back to the truck.

"Can I talk to you privately?" Nate put an arm around Cliff's shoulders and waved at the small crowd with his other arm—the crowd that had grown from five for the last game to seven now. "Hang on, guys. Just give me a sec."

Sandra kept trying to creep closer, and as she did, Nate led the pastor away. She realized she was being painfully obvious, but threw that concern to the wind—she'd already gotten the reputation of being a snoop, right? She strained to hear, but couldn't make out the pastor's defense, only snippets of her husband's persuasion. "You've got to know that's a silly rule ... you can't force someone to go to church ... they don't even know the rules yet ... do you want the community to think we're snobs?" She didn't know if Nate convinced him or just wore him out, but with about thirty seconds till the first pitch, Cliff surrendered, and Nate waved the men onto the field. "Sorry about the confusion!"

"Can I pitch this game?" Ton Truck asked again.

Cliff either didn't hear him or ignored him.

"Probably not," Nate said, sounding embarrassed. "Let me work on that for you."

"He's really good. Better than ..." Adam's voice trailed off as he looked out at the field. "Better than most."

Nate snickered. "I'm sure of it."

The pastor assigned the positions and then New Hope took the field.

Pastor threw the first pitch and it floated toward home plate. The batter had time for three swings between release and the ball entering the strike zone, but he only swung once—a perfectly timed swing that sent a line drive right at the third basemen. Sandra's immediate thought was, *That is going to break Brendan's face.* But Brendan wasn't there. A

Bickford was, and he caught it effortlessly and tossed it back to the open-mouthed pitcher, who promptly dropped it. The bleachers burst into cheers. Who could blame them? They'd never seen anyone stop a line drive before—no one from New Hope could catch a line drive, and no one from New Hope could hit a line drive so that the other team could catch one.

Chapter 26

The Bickfords could hit line drives. They could also hit home runs, sacrifice flies, and grounders up the third base line. It took Sandra a few innings to figure out that they were actually placing their hits on purpose. It took Faith Community the same amount of time to try a different pitcher, but that didn't slow New Hope down an iota.

At the end of the third inning, the score was twelve to two. The two runs that New Hope had given up were home runs that went over the fence—hence, the Bickfords couldn't field them. Sandra had a feeling that if Ton Truck had been pitching, they'd be on their way to a shutout. But, the situation was what it was, and she had no skin in the game. It was just fun watching the Bickfords play. It was like a real sport.

During the bottom of the fourth, a giant black Toyota Sequoia pulled into the parking lot. The tinted windows prevented Sandra from knowing exactly who was inside, but she would know that vehicle anywhere. The vanity plates read: CATVAC2. Though there was hardly enough room, the driver nosed the giant vehicle in directly behind the bleachers. Sandra wondered if a Bickford could aim a pop fly to smash that windshield. The new angle allowed her to see that Brendan was driving, and soon they all spilled out of the vehicle. The kids ran ahead of Daphne and scampered up into the bleachers. Daphne was moving more slowly, and her smudged eye makeup suggested she'd been crying. Sandra's heart ached for her. She couldn't imagine what she was going through. What do you tell your children when their grandfather has been arrested for killing a stranger? She vowed to reach out to Daphne, no matter what weird staring contest they'd had on Sunday.

Brendan strode up to Pastor Cliff and made no effort to avoid being overheard. "I thought you said these guys couldn't play."

Pastor Cliff gave him a grave look and then walked away.

"Hey!" Brendan cried, looking appalled. "I'm talking to you!"

Nate went over and put a hand on Brendan's shoulder, which he promptly shook off. "Don't touch me. You're the one who invited this trash."

Nate was still talking when Brendan walked away from him, as Pastor Cliff had just done to him, and chased after his pastor. "Put me in the game," he demanded.

Pastor turned only his head to look at Brendan. His body stayed facing away. "I will, next inning."

"No." Brendan stepped closer. "*Now.*"

Shocking Sandra, Cliff laughed at him. For a second, Sandra was certain Brendan was going to hit the pastor, but then he seemed to get control of himself and came into the dugout. Sandra held her breath. She could feel the anger rolling off him in waves of heat, and she pulled the stroller closer to her. Now she was *really* glad the Bickfords had shown up, so that Peter wasn't allowed to go out onto the field with this man. Also because if Brendan got violent and decided to go after somebody else with an old bat, she was certain the Bickfords could take him.

As promised, Pastor Cliff put Brendan into the game when New Hope took the field again, and it didn't take long for Faith Community to figure out that the third base line was now the spot to shoot for. They fouled off a lot of pitches, leaving Pastor Cliff holding his lower back between offerings, but the ones that stayed fair promised them base runners. Though the short fielder played directly behind Brendan, it was still too much of a throw to first base.

And so, slowly but surely, Faith Community crept back into the game. At the bottom of the sixth, Ton Truck again pleaded for reason. "Come on, man. I can end this."

Pastor Cliff pretended not to hear him. "This game is just for fun. It's not about winning and losing."

Of course it's not about winning if you insist on throwing every pitch. Sandra was a little embarrassed at how annoyed she was with the whole thing, and hoped no one could tell. Peter had taken Joanna to the playground, and she was grateful—her kids always knew when she was annoyed.

"Is it always this dramatic?" Ethel asked.

"No. The drama has definitely picked up since the Bickfords came aboard."

Lewis barked for the lineup, which was extra ridiculous this time since he wasn't in it. Maybe he thought Pastor had put him in the game without telling him.

Nevertheless, Sandra dutifully called out the lineup, taking a silent thrill in the fact that the next four batters were Bickfords.

Chapter 27

It was a squeaker, but thanks to the Bickford family, New Hope was victorious over Faith Community. Everyone celebrated except for Pastor Cliff, who pretended he did not care. Or maybe he truly didn't. Sandra didn't know.

"Can you hang out here for another second?" she whispered to Ethel. "I'm going to go talk to Daphne."

"You mean you're going to go snoop?"

Sandra grinned.

"Go, go, of course." Ethel waved her away from the stroller and then engaged Sammy in a game of peekaboo.

Sandra made a beeline for Daphne, before she could get away. She sat down in front of her on the bleachers and tried to give her a sincere smile. "I'm so sorry for all that you're going through—"

"Save it. I know who you are, that you like to pretend to be a detective, and I'm not telling you anything."

Whoah. "I'm sorry?"

It was difficult to read her expression through her giant sunglasses. Had she put those glasses on to hide the fact that she'd been crying? "Just mind your own business!"

"Daphne, I'm just trying to be kind here. I'm truly—"

She stood up abruptly. "You've never been kind to me before. Now my father-in-law kills someone and we're suddenly besties? I hardly think so." She grabbed her daughter's arm and began to pull her out of the bleachers.

Sandra stood too and stepped in front of her. She lowered her voice. "You just said he killed someone. Do you really think that?

Because I don't." She leaned closer to the frigid woman. "I want to *help* Richard."

Daphne pushed her aside with such force that Sandra almost toppled sideways out of the bleachers. "And I'm telling you that we don't want or need your help!" She raised her chin and directed her voice out onto the field. "Yes, it's true!" she cried out, her voice stronger than Sandra ever would have imagined it could be. "My father-in-law, Richard Barney, is an evil man. Always has been! So, now you all know!"

Brendan came running at his wife with fire in his eyes. If she saw him coming, she didn't care. The girl in her clutch started to cry, but Sandra didn't know if it was from her mother's grip or her horrific words. Sandra headed toward them with the intent of grabbing the child out of that painful grasp.

"You can all say what you want about him! I don't care! We'll be moving away from all you ignorant hicks soon enough—"

Sandra reached them at the same time as Brendan, and in the end, didn't need to do anything, because when Brendan grabbed for his wife, she promptly let go of her daughter. He hissed something into her ear and then dragged her toward the SUV with such force that it jostled her glasses off her face. Her girls trailed behind her and the oldest one stooped to pick up the glasses as she walked by—notably unrattled by her circumstances.

The field was completely silent. Those who had already headed for their cars peppered the parking lot. They were half-changed out of their sweats, standing there with their trunks open or their fingers on their door handles—the entire scene had frozen when Daphne had delivered her diatribe, and no one seemed to know how to thaw it. Pastor Cliff slunk away with his duffel bag over his shoulder.

Suddenly, Bob appeared directly behind Sandra. She started to whirl around. He grabbed her elbow to steady her. "Don't look at me."

She nodded her understanding and muttered through closed teeth. "Did you hear all that?"

"Sure did. *Now* do you think he's guilty?"

"Sure don't."

Bob chuckled, a response she still found rewarding. Making an angel laugh never got old. "I wonder if these people are ever going to leave? Are they hoping for more of a show?"

At first, she didn't say anything. She pretended to scratch her nose so she could cover her mouth while she spoke. "I'm not sure, and I'm not sure how to make them leave."

The lightning was so bright it hurt her eyes, and simultaneous thunder cracked so loudly that everyone jumped. Sandra almost fell out of the bleachers again, but Bob grabbed her to steady her. The heavens started gushing rain before she'd figured out what was happening. Everyone sprang into action, grabbed their children, their gear, and their lawn furniture and rushed for cover—including Ethel, who came toward her pushing the stroller over the uneven ground.

Sandra found her voice. "Did you just make this happen?" But when she turned to look at Bob, he was gone again. She ran toward Ethel and grabbed the stroller. "I'm so sorry!"

"Don't be sorry! You didn't make it rain!"

But hadn't she? Sort of? "Thank you so much for your help! I owe you huge!"

"You don't owe me a thing!" At least, that's what Sandra thought she said, as the tail end of her statement was carried away by the wind that had come from nowhere and was now blowing Sandra toward her minivan. She squinted through the downpour to check the swing set, but her kids weren't there. *Oh no.* Her panicked eyes checked the distance to the van and were so grateful to see that Peter and Joanna were closer to it than she was. Peter was dragging Joanna by one arm, and Joanna didn't even look mad about it. They jumped into the van and then the van started to move. For one panicked second, Sandra thought her husband had forgotten about Sammy and her, but then she realized he was coming for her.

He stopped right in front of her. "Grab Sammy and get in the front!" he hollered. "Forget the car seat! I'll get the stroller." She did as she was told, and as she climbed into the front, she felt the wind from the back gate being open. The van had become a wind tunnel. She looked back at Ethel. "Get in the back! We'll drive you to your car!" She slammed the front door.

Joanna moved to the way back of the van to make room for Ethel as she climbed in. Then Nate shut the liftgate and the van became a quiet refuge—a quiet that was interrupted when Nate opened the driver's side door to throw himself inside. But then he shut it again and placed his hands on the steering wheel as he caught his breath. "What was *that*?" he finally said.

"What do you mean? Daphne's announcement or the storm?" Sandra handed Sammy back to Peter. "Can you strap him in, honey, so I don't drown trying?" Then she looked at her husband, waiting for an answer.

"Both, I guess."

"I'm not sure."

He looked at her, and his bangs dripped into his eyes. "I didn't see any clouds beforehand."

She didn't know what to say. Was Nate accusing Bob? "Yeah, but we were all fixated on the game and then on Daphne's little performance."

"What performance?" Peter asked. "What did she do?"

"I'll tell you later," Sandra said dismissively.

"No, you won't," he griped.

She turned to look at him. "No, I really will. I like having your help with my cases."

Nate gave her a dirty look which made her laugh, and her laughter made her kids laugh, which made Ethel laugh. Then even Nate had to laugh.

"I guess these storms can just come out of nowhere sometimes," Sandra said.

His smile faded. "But it wasn't even hot enough for a thunderstorm, and we didn't get any warnings on our phones?"

She really wanted him to drop it. She knew from experience that she was never going to know who made the storm come or why. She doubted Bob had that kind of juice, but if he did, and if he'd used it, he was never going to admit it.

"Can you please drive Ethel to her car?"

"Yes, of course." He put the minivan in drive.

"Maybe the angels are crying about the man who died," Joanna said in her softest voice.

Nate adjusted the rearview so he could see his only daughter's precious eyes. "You know what, honey? I bet you're right. I bet that's exactly what happened."

Chapter 28

With the kids tucked into bed, Sandra nestled into the couch near Nate. The television was on, but he was mostly paying attention to his phone. "The rain stopped," she said, trying to get a conversation going.

"Mm-hmm." He did not look up.

She stared at the television for a few minutes but couldn't make herself focus enough to figure out what was going on on the screen. "So, what did you think of Daphne's outburst?"

"Mm-hmm."

She stared at him for a second and then cleared her throat.

He finally looked up at her. "What?"

"I asked you a question."

"What?"

She considered strangling him, but she liked him too much. "I asked what you thought about Daphne's outburst?"

He let out a slow breath and returned his eyes to his phone. His thumb began to swipe up. "Honestly? The whole bunch of them scare me a little, and I'd rather not think about them at all."

"The whole bunch of who?"

"The Barneys."

She found it amusing that her husband was more comfortable around the Bickfords than the Barneys. "I don't think they're all bad."

He snorted. "Really? I've never heard you say a nice thing about them."

"Well, I like the kids."

He laughed a genuine laugh, and her chest swelled with happiness. She loved to make him laugh.

"But really, I know Brendan isn't very pleasant, maybe a bit arrogant, but that doesn't mean that Richard is a murderer."

"I never said he was a murderer," he mumbled. "I just said they scare me a little."

She was finally frustrated. "What on that phone could possibly be more interesting than one of our neighbors being accused of murder?"

With a straight face he turned the screen of his phone so that she could see it. "I'm a zombie and I'm trying not to get hit by a train in the subway." His boyish expression suggested that he thought she would find this cute and amusing.

She did not. "Do you think he did it?"

He put the phone down, dramatically, making it clear that he was now engaging in this conversation against his will. His eyes settled on the television. It took her a full minute to locate the remote control and press the mute button.

"Seriously?"

"Seriously. I am asking you to talk to me without watching television at the same time. So? What do you think?"

"I told you. I don't know!"

She thought about easing off, letting him slip back into his mind's nothing box. She didn't want to exasperate him. "I just don't think Richard did it. It doesn't make any sense. And the fact that Daphne was so willing to publicly declare his guilt makes me more suspicious. I think she's try to cover for her husband. Or maybe she did it."

Nate tipped his head back and laughed at the ceiling. This time, the laughter was not encouraging. This time he wasn't laughing because he thought she was charming and funny. This time he was laughing *at* her.

"What?" She sat up straighter, ready to defend herself.

"Nothing. I just don't think Daphne could hurt a fly. She's like the perfect trophy wife. I've never seen anyone so put together. Her kids never even have wrinkles in their clothes."

She scowled. Was he criticizing her? She wasn't sure. "You mean, she reminds you of a Stepford wife?"

He looked at her. "Huh?"

"Never mind. Just go back to television." He had a point, though. She didn't think Daphne would risk breaking a nail in order to bludgeon someone with a bat.

Nate squiggled closer to her and put a hand on her knee. "We can watch something else if you want to pick a show. It's not that I don't want to talk to you. I just don't know what's going on and I find the whole topic morbid. It makes me feel kind of helpless knowing that a murder happened practically in our own backyard. Can we dwell on something else?"

She thought about it for a minute and then gave up. She loved her husband, but he was no Bob. She was grateful God had sent her a different partner for sleuthing. But, where was this partner now? She turned her own eyes back to the TV and even though she didn't bother to try to follow the story, the flickering bright lights were oddly relaxing.

Within fifteen minutes, her husband started snoring softly beside her. She glanced at him and his eyes were still open. Talk about creepy. She grabbed a nearby afghan, gently covered him up, and then slowly stood, taking care not to wake him. When she looked back down, his eyes had slipped shut. She went through her back door, sat down on the back steps, and looked up at the night sky. Plainfield was a small enough town that there wasn't much light pollution and she could see thousands of stars, not nearly as many as she knew were there, but plenty enough to wow her. She wondered where Bob was. She wanted to further discuss Daphne's outburst. But did she even need to discuss it with him? She knew how she felt about it. No one acted like that. If Daphne truly thought Richard was guilty, wouldn't she be embarrassed? Wouldn't she be quieter about it? The only reason Sandra could come up with to publicly spout such venom was that Daphne was trying to divert attention away from the person who was actually guilty, which was either her husband or herself. It was easier for Sandra to picture Brendon being the killer than it was to picture Daphne swinging a bat in the woods in her perfectly pressed slacks, but Daphne was the one who'd had the outburst—not Brendan. She put her head in her hands. This was too much. She needed to stop thinking about it and just let the police work it out.

TobyMac started belting out "Speak Life," and Sandra scrambled to her feet and ran inside, letting the screen door bang shut behind her. In the quiet house, it sounded like a gunshot. *Please don't wake Sammy, please don't wake Sammy.* She lunged for her phone and answered it before Toby could start the chorus over again. "Hello?" She tried to catch her breath.

The line was silent.

"Hello?" she said again, more loudly.

Still nothing.

She pulled the phone away from her ear and looked at it to see who was calling. It was a Maine number, but she didn't recognize it. It was after ten o'clock. Who on earth was calling her and why weren't they saying anything? A chill ran across her shoulders. "Hello? Is anyone there?"

She thought she heard a faint whimper, but just as quickly worried she had imagined it. "Hello? Are you okay?"

More silence.

She pulled the phone away again and saw that the call had ended. The timer on her phone was no longer running. What on earth? With quick, practiced fingers that almost rivaled the dexterity of her technically advanced eleven-year-old son, Sandra pasted the mystery number into the search box. Within three seconds, she learned that the digits belonged to Hope House of Lewiston, Maine. Her breath caught. Someone had called her from Hope House? It was Tiara. It had to be. But what was she going to do about it?

She looked at the clock again as if some part of her wished it had just miraculously become daylight and a reasonable hour to pay a visit to Hope House. But of course, it remained the middle of the night. She couldn't call Hope House back, because she would get the front desk, wouldn't she? It wasn't like she had a direct line to Tiara's room. She groaned in frustration. The girl had actually called her, but Sandra couldn't do anything about it. She collapsed in her kitchen chair and put her head on the table. What a bummer.

An inch away from her head Toby started singing again, and she jumped so efficiently that she rapped her knee on the underside of the table. She cried out just as she answered the phone, so her hello sounded a bit like a cat being forced into a Cat Vac. She forced herself to lower her voice to a more reasonable register and said hello again.

This time, someone spoke. "Hi. It's Tiara, Phoenix's friend."

Chapter 29

"Tiara, hi!" she cried, too late realizing she sounded far too excited. She forced herself to wait for Tiara to speak.

Finally, she did. "I wasn't sure if I should call ... I'm still not sure."

Sandra hesitated, making sure not to talk over her. "I'm glad you did."

"I just can't stop thinking about him." Her voice cracked. "I'm not even sure if I want to know what happened to him. But it's just not fair. He was just getting his life together, and then they did this to him."

"Who did this to him?"

"I don't know," she said quickly.

"You just said *they*." Sandra realized she was pushing and made herself stop.

"Well, yeah, I just meant *they*, you know, like someone. I don't know who. Really, I don't. If I did, of course I would tell you. I don't want someone to get away with it."

Then why had she called? Just to talk to someone about Phoenix? Sandra was disappointed, but she would also do this for her, if that's with this young woman needed. "I'm so sorry, Tiara. I can't imagine what you're going through."

She chuckled dryly. "I can't imagine it either, and I'm living it. I mean, I hadn't known Phoenix for very long, but it felt like a long time. He was going to be a great guy. He was just figuring out who he was, and he really liked me. He was so sweet. No one has ever been that nice to me."

Sandra's heart cracked.

"Anyway, I don't know if it's any good, but I thought of something. And I don't want to stir up drama, so don't tell anyone where you got this, and if you do, I will swear that I don't know anything. I don't want to talk to no cops."

"Okay. What is it?"

She inhaled sharply. "I think I know why he was in Plainfield."

Sandra's whole body went still, as if the slightest movement or noise might scare this information off. After a long pause, she prodded, "Why?"

"Ever since Phoenix got sober, he's been obsessed with finding his father."

His father? Another chill danced across her shoulders.

"I mean, he had a father. Phoenix's stepdad adopted him a long time ago, so it's not like Phoenix was some helpless orphan or anything. It's just that, he said that he almost died not ever knowing who his father was, and he wasn't going to let that happen. He wanted to know him, because he learned that addiction runs in families, and he wanted to know if his dad was an addict. I think that he thought he wanted to help him, like if his dad was an addict, Phoenix was going to save him. I don't know."

Sandra gave this information a minute to settle into a straight line in her brain and then said, "And you think Phoenix found his biological father?"

"I don't know for sure, but yeah, Phoenix said that he thought he'd found him. He didn't tell me he was going to go see him, though, so I don't know if that's what was happening, and he didn't tell me his name. He just told me that he found him, and he was all secretive about it. And he didn't seem really excited. Like, he didn't really like what he'd found."

It had to be Richard, but why wouldn't Phoenix be excited to learn that Richard was his father? Sure, Richard was kind of a jerk, but had

Phoenix figured that out that quickly? "Do you know when exactly that he figured it out?"

"He told me a few days before he died."

Sandra gasped. Tiara was right—the two things were connected. No way did he just happen to discover who his father was and then get killed for some other random reason two days later. "And he didn't tell you *why* he wasn't excited?"

Tiara exhaled loudly into the phone, and Sandra realized she was probably smoking a cigarette. "I don't know. Maybe he was happy about it, I don't know. He just seemed like maybe this guy was going to be hard to get to. Like ... I really don't know, but if it was the man that they arrested? He's like really rich, right? So maybe Phoenix was worried that he wouldn't be able to talk to him? But I don't know. I don't want to start anything."

"And he didn't tell you anything else about the man he'd found?"

"Naw ... nothin'." She paused. "That's why I wasn't sure if I should tell you. But then they arrested a rich guy and it just sort of clicked in my head. Maybe that's why Phoenix acted weird, because his bio dad was like untouchable or something."

Sandra rolled her eyes. It wasn't like he was Al Capone—the man had invented a cat hair vacuum. "Do you know *how* he figured it out?"

"No idea," she said quickly. "He spent a lot of time on the computer at the library. And I know he called some of his mom's old friends."

Maybe Bob and she *should* have gone to see Phoenix's parents after all.

"His mom is dead now, though, so she couldn't have told him."

Or not.

"So anyway, I gotta go, but I thought, you know, maybe you could find out if he is really the bio dad, and if he is, maybe tell the cops. But keep me out of it, for real."

"I will, Tiara. Thanks so much for ..." Sandra realized she could no longer hear Tiara breathing, and she looked at the phone's screen to verify that yes, Tiara had hung up on her. She put the phone down and sat there a minute letting all that sink in. No, she had no way to know whether what Tiara had told her was significant or even true. And yet, she knew it was both. Richard Barney was Phoenix's father. Phoenix had come to Plainfield to meet him, or maybe just to check him out from afar. No safer place to do that than a church softball game.

So, who had killed him? Maybe Richard really was to blame. Or maybe Brendan didn't want to share his inheritance. She thought that was a far more likely scenario.

Chapter 30

Now she really needed to talk to Bob. But how? Did she need to get shoved into a trunk and chased into a forest before he'd check in? Not for the first time, she wished Bob had a cell phone.

She could ask God to send Bob her way, but she didn't want to bother the Almighty with her amateur sleuthing when she wasn't even sure if he approved of it. She returned to her perch on the back step and looked up at the stars again. "Bob?" she called out softly, feeling beyond foolish. "Are you out there?" Maybe she should go hang out with the chickadees. He liked them. But she didn't know where they were right now either.

"I'm here."

She jumped. He was standing right beside her steps, and even though she had been requesting his presence, she obviously hadn't been expecting it, because now her heart was trying to stomp its way out of her chest. "You scared me!"

He chuckled. "Sorry. I have that effect on humans. So, I have news." He sat down beside her, but there wasn't quite enough room on the steps so he pushed her over to give himself more space. Now a third of her bottom hung out over the edge of the step, and she wondered how bizarre that would look to anyone who might be spying on her in her backyard. No one sat like this. Ever.

"I have news!" he said again.

She could feel the energy vibrating off him. "Really? Are you going to make me beg?"

He chuckled. "No. I did some snooping, and I think I figured out a motive. I think Richard Barney is Phoenix's father."

She gasped.

He looked at her, his eyes wide. "I know, crazy, right?" He was obviously quite proud of himself.

She laughed. "And how did you come to this conclusion?"

"I asked around, and found out that Phoenix's mother knew Richard." He coughed. "She knew him well."

"And how did you figure this out?"

"I told you. I asked around."

"You asked around with humans or with angels?"

He ignored this question. "The point is, maybe Phoenix was in Plainfield to confront his father. You were at the softball game that he played in, right? Did it look like they knew each other?"

Sandra tried to think back. She wasn't sure the word "play" was apt to describe what Phoenix had done during that game, but it was probably technically correct. He had stood on the field with a glove on his hand. "I don't remember much. I was trying to watch the game and keep score, but no, I never saw Phoenix talk to anyone. And I don't think Richard knew who he was. If Richard's illegitimate son was on the field and he knew about it, then he would have tried to stop that from happening. I think he would have found that embarrassing. I mean, doesn't Richard Barney really care what people think?"

Bob shrugged. "I have no idea."

"Well I'm telling you, I haven't known him for very long, but I'm certain that he cares what people think."

Bob stared off into the distance and nodded. "Okay then. But doesn't Brendan care too?"

"Yes, I've thought the same thing. I think Brendan's our guy, not Richard. And you're not the only one who has done some sleuthing tonight."

He looked at her with one eyebrow cocked. "Oh, really? Are you jealous that I just broke the case wide open?"

She rocked back laughing and then felt self-conscious. "No one can see us right now, right? Because my butt's hanging halfway off the step, and I'm talking to myself and laughing at the stars."

"No, no one is looking." He sounded impatient with her human concerns. "So, what sleuthing did you do?"

"Tiara called," she said, only a little sad that Bob had effectively stolen her thunder.

"And, what did she say?"

"I was going to tell you, if you'd let me. She said the same thing you said. Well, she didn't say that Richard Barney was the father, but she did say that Phoenix had just recently figured out who his father was—in fact, just a few days before he died."

Bob gasped. "So we're right. Brendan's the killer."

"I don't know. Or Daphne."

Bob laughed as if that was ridiculous, and Sandra was sick of all the beings in her life acting as though it was impossible for perfect Daphne to swing a bat. She forcefully swallowed her pride. "You're right, it's probably Brendan. I don't think he wanted to share his inheritance."

"Yes, it does seem that a cat hair vacuum is worth a lot of money."

"So, should we call Chip and Slaughter?"

"Maybe." Bob paused for so long that Sandra wondered if he had nodded off. "Or maybe we could try to bait Daphne ourselves."

"*Bait* her?" She wasn't sure she liked the sound of that. "What does that mean, exactly?"

He shrugged. "I'm not sure yet, but I wouldn't think it would be that hard. I am certain she knows who the killer is, but I don't think she's much of a criminal mastermind. And she's obviously volatile. So let's use that to our advantage. If we somehow let her know what we know, then maybe she would admit something to us or in front of us." He looked at her. "Well, I mean, in front of you."

Sandra thought about it but was skeptical. "I don't know ..."

"We don't even have to do it in person. Let's just send a note. Tell her we know that Richard is Phoenix's father."

"No!" Sandra cried. "Then she tells her crazy husband, and he kills someone else!"

"Who else would he kill?"

"I don't know—maybe the stupid woman who sent his volatile wife a note!"

Bob laughed, which seemed a strange response to Sandra's fear. "You get shoved in one trunk and now you're all about playing it safe." He stared out into the darkness of her backyard again. "I just feel like we need to do something, something to shake things up. I think she's excitable, and if we get her excited, then I think she'll make a mistake and say too much."

"And you're basing all this on one emotional bleacher outburst?"

"Oh no," he said quickly. "There's more than that. Think about the way she was watching you in church. There was fury in her eyes, a fury she seemed to be fighting to contain. And she may have every reason to have fury, if she's married to a murderer. I'm telling you, we just need a catalyst."

They sat in a comfortable silence for several minutes, each scheming. "You want an explosion?" Sandra said, only partly taking herself seriously. "Then let's come at them with more than just the paternity. Let's say we have the church video footage."

"But we don't."

She gave him a devious smile. "She doesn't know that."

He looked at her sternly. "We can't lie."

"I'm not *lying*. I'm *bluffing*. They do it in law enforcement all the time."

"Bluffing *is* lying."

Oddly, his resistance to the idea made her more enthusiastic about it. "I'm not sure I was asking your permission, Bob!"

"Okay, let's say you're going to do this." He'd suddenly removed himself from the equation. "How do you deliver the message?"

"Anonymously, obviously."

"Right. And look how well that turned out last time you tried to be anonymous."

The fire phone fiasco. "Good point."

"I think she could, with very little effort, trace the message back to you."

Maybe this wasn't a good idea. "All right. Never mind."

"I'll do it."

Her head snapped up. "What? You'll do what?"

"You write the note. Anonymously. I'll deliver it, and then I'll watch and tell you what she does."

Sandra was jealous. "I want to see what she does!"

"Okay, we'll put it on her windshield then." He smiled at her. "You go get some sleep. I'll come by tomorrow, and I'll go put the note on her windshield. Then we'll wait and watch."

"I'll have the kids tomorrow!"

"Then you'd better call Ethel." And poof, again, no more Bob.

Chapter 31

"**I** have the videos," Sandra wrote with a shaky hand. Despite Bob's instructions, she hadn't gone to bed. Like she was going to be able to sleep now. She moved that paper aside and started again on the fresh sheet beneath. "*We* have the videos," she wrote. "We" sounded much more ominous than "I." It would be harder for Daphne to send her murderous husband to kill a whole team of snoops.

She chewed on the end of her pencil. Now what?

"Turn yourself in, or we give them to the police." She smiled. Not bad. That was a fairly persuasive piece of poetry.

Except, who was "yourself," exactly? Why would Daphne turn *herself* in if her *husband* was the killer? Should she write, "Turn your husband in" instead? Nah, because if Daphne *had* done it, then that just proved they didn't know what they were talking about. They didn't have the videos. A bluff only worked if it sounded real. Duh.

She tossed aside that draft and got a new sheet, wrote "We have the videos" again, and then pressed the tip of her mechanical Bic to the page and waited for inspiration.

It struck. "Do the right thing, or we give them to the police."

Perfect.

A little bizarre, because who wouldn't just give the videos to the police in the first place without baiting a murderer, but oh well. Someone who wanted a piece of the action, that's who.

Satisfied, Sandra neatly folded the page, put it in her purse, set the timer on the coffee pot, and then finally went to bed.

She awoke only a few hours later to a maroon-faced Nate shaking her shoulder. "Wh ... wh ... what?" She rubbed her eyes. "What's the matter? The kids—"

"The kids are fine," Nate snapped. She didn't think she'd ever seen him so mad, and his anger scared her. She sat up. "Nate, what is it, tell me, you're scaring me."

He sat down on the bed beside her. "I'm scaring you? You've got to be kidding me. I'm the one who should be scared."

She was so confused. She needed coffee, but she thought telling him this would make matters worse. "Honey, please slow down. I don't understand." Then she noticed the piece of paper clutched in his hand, and everything became clear. "You went through my purse?"

"I needed the nail clippers!" he cried as if his violation of her nonexistent privacy was the last detail that they needed to be focusing on right now. "What is this?" He shook his hand, and the paper crackled in his clutch.

She realized she was going to have to rewrite it. She didn't want to deliver a crumpled bluff. "Honey, don't worry. It's perfectly safe. It was Bob's idea."

He bounced off the bed. "Bob's idea? Where did Bob come from? Have you guys been sneaking around behind my back investigating this thing?" He didn't allow her to answer that question. "You promised you were going to stay out of this!"

She had promised that, hadn't she? And she'd even almost meant it at the time. "Honey, I'm sorry. I have stayed out of it—mostly. And I'm not getting terribly involved this time. But Daphne knows more than she's telling, so we thought it would be a good idea if we stirred the pot a little."

He put his hands on his hips and glowered at her as if he couldn't quite believe what he was seeing. "Stir the pot," he repeated. "You can't be serious."

"Yes, but it's no big deal. I'll be with Bob, and he won't let anything happen to me."

"*Be* with Bob? What do you mean? Be with him where? What is the plan?"

She really needed coffee. "We're going to put that note under her sixty-thousand dollar windshield and then we're just going to watch, and see if she freaks out."

"Of course she's going to freak out. Maybe even more so if she's innocent. This is a pretty creepy note to receive if you haven't done anything wrong." He was sounding less irate and more curious.

"Well, we're hoping she does something stupid that will incriminate her. If she's innocent, and we cause her undeserved grief, then we'll apologize later. But she's not innocent."

Nate shook his head. "She's probably not completely innocent. But she's not the murderer."

"So you guys keep telling me."

Nate smirked. "Bob doesn't think she did it, either?"

She rolled her eyes and flopped back down onto the bed. "No. You guys don't think a woman with perfect hair is capable of the criminal life."

Nate tilted his head to the side and gave her a peeved look. "I never said anything about the woman's hair. That would be weird."

She snickered. "Yes it would. You're right. Honey, I'm sorry that I didn't tell you, but I promise, this isn't a big deal. We're going to help solve this thing, and I will be with Bob the whole time, and I will be perfectly safe."

"You're not going unless I go."

Her eyes snapped toward him. "What? No!"

"Yes. I think it's about time I meet this Bob fella."

Chapter 32

Nate poured Sandra a third cup of coffee. "Are you sure he didn't give you a time?"

For the third time, Sandra said no. "He's an angel, Nate. I try not to make demands of him and boss him around. He said he was going to show up and I'm grateful he's going to show up, so I didn't nail down a time."

He gave her side eye. "You don't need to be terse with me. You're the one in the wrong here, don't forget."

She looked down at her cup. She wasn't going to argue with him, but she didn't think she was in the wrong at all. She was trying to be a hero. There was a crash from the living room but neither of them looked. Ethel was in there with the children, and if one of them went rushing in there, they would only mess with her methodology.

Nate sat down across from her and leaned back in the chair. "So, we wait."

"Yes, like I said. We be patient."

"And he's not just going to show up invisible and whisk you away without my knowledge?"

She snickered. "He may be here right now and be invisible and be furious that I've told you the plan. But I don't know if he can make me invisible." She figured that he probably could, but she wasn't going to tell Nate that.

"I can't believe I'm the last one to meet him."

"You're not. Joanna still hasn't met him yet."

"That we know of."

Sandra snickered. This was true. Joanna could have been chatting with him for months. She had lots of invisible friends.

"Sandra?" Bob said slowly.

She looked around the room but couldn't see him. "Yes?"

"Yes, what?" Nate said. "Is he here? Is that him?"

"What's going on?" Bob said just as slowly.

"I'm sorry, Bob. I didn't mean to complicate things. My wonderful husband here found my bluff note in my purse. He wants to go with us on our mission—"

"But first, I want to see you!"

Sandra found Nate's tone a bit too demanding for an angel.

Apparently, Bob thought so too because he didn't appear. "I'm not sure that's a good idea. The more people who go, the harder it will be to hide."

"Well? What's he saying?" It was obvious that Nate did not appreciate the suspense.

"He says that it's not a good idea to take a bunch of people on this particular mission. We're trying to be discreet."

"Stop calling it a mission! You're going to drop a note off. And it's not a bunch of people! It's your husband!"

Bob appeared right beside the table. "You make a good point, sir."

Nate let out a little shriek as he pushed his chair back away from the angel. The squawk of cheap furniture on flooring almost harmonized with the shriek that came out of his mouth. Then he froze and stared at the heavenly being in front of him. He opened his mouth but no sound came out.

Sandra wondered if she had acted this shocked during her first encounter. She didn't think she had. She knew Peter and Ethel hadn't. And Sammy, well, Sammy hadn't even blinked. "Honey, this is Bob. Bob, this is honey." She laughed at the charm of her introduction.

Nate did not laugh. He still hadn't moved. Finally, he said, "You're ... you?"

Huh? Her husband was cracking under the pressure. He couldn't even use words. She got up and rounded the table to take his hand. "It's okay. I know it's a lot, at first, but you'll get used to him."

"He's just ... not what I was expecting."

Bob furrowed his brow in obvious offense.

"I thought you'd be ... bigger ... and—"

"Okay, enough about that." She looked at Bob. "Thanks for appearing to him. So, what's the plan?"

Bob looked at Nate. "You really want to be a part of this?"

"Honestly?" Nate spoke slowly, as if he had to work to push out each syllable individually. "I'm not sure, but I don't want my wife doing this unless I go to protect her."

Bob looked offended again. "I'm pretty sure I can protect her."

Nate stood up and puffed out his chest. "But she's my wife."

Bob held up both hands. "Of course. I have no designs on her in that way. I didn't mean to suggest—"

"We know that," Nate interrupted, his tone softening. "I didn't mean to suggest that either. I'm just saying that I want to be there. If she's there, I should be there. There's no such thing as too much protection."

Sandra wasn't sure this was true and thought about letting Bob go off and leave the note by himself, but she didn't want to miss anything. "Okay, so I ask again, what is the plan?"

Bob took a deep breath. "I see that Ethel is here. Perfect. Right now, Daphne is home, and her vehicle is parked out front—"

"Where does she live, exactly?" Nate asked.

"At the end of a very long driveway on Osborne Hill Road."

"In the new housing development?"

Sandra tried to shush him with her eyes. Did he really need an address at this point?

"Is that near where Richard lives?"

Bob narrowed his eyes. "They all live in the same house."

"Really?" Nate looked incredulous.

Sandra couldn't imagine why he cared so much.

"It's a *really* big house," Bob said. "And I don't know how long she'll be there, so we should get going." He stared at them expectantly.

Sandra grabbed her purse and headed for the door. When she reached for the doorknob, she realized her husband hadn't moved. Vaguely, she wondered if it was wrong how unenthusiastic she felt about his joining her unofficial detective agency. She looked back at him and tried not to sound snippy when she said, "Are you coming?"

"How does this work, exactly?" he asked, still not moving his feet.

How does *what* work, exactly? And when had her brilliant husband become so daft?

No one answered him, so he clarified, "How do we get there?"

Did he think they were going to fly? She held up the keys. "We take the minivan."

His feet began to move then, and his eyes dropped to watch them. "Oh, okay."

Chapter 33

For several reasons, Sandra wasn't thrilled when Bob instructed Nate to park behind an abandoned chicken barn a mile away from the Barney mansion. First, though the chicken barn had long ago bid adieu to its last chicken resident, it still smelled nightmarish, and she feared the stench would stick to her beloved minivan. Second, she wasn't in the mood for a long walk through the woods with her husband. And third, it wasn't soccer season and she was a bit out of shape, so she didn't really want to take a long walk at all.

Bob must have sensed some of this, as he promised to begin the journey with them. He led the way through the forest, and it wasn't smooth going. This wasn't a maintained path through a state park. This was a thicket. She had to be circumspect with just about every step, lest she roll an ankle, get her foot caught, trip, fall off a cliff, step on a hornets' nest, kick a baby black bear, or some simultaneous combination of the aforementioned. And though she was focused mostly on her feet, her arms were doing some crazy version of the salsa dance as she tried to ward off swarms of rabid mosquitoes. The only comfort was that her darling husband seemed to be having just as much trouble: the more he slapped himself in the face, the harder she had to work not to laugh at him.

Finally, Bob told them to pause. "We're almost there," he whispered. It wasn't fair. He didn't seem out of breath, and hadn't been assaulted by a single mosquito. Did mosquitoes not eat angels?

"Just past those trees," he said, as if she could possibly know which trees he meant. All she could see was trees in all directions, "there is a clearing. That is their land, but don't worry, they can't see you from the house. But we'll cross the clearing, and there will be a hedge that lines their driveway. If you go past that hedge, the security cameras will be able to pick you up—"

"They have security cameras?" Nate cried and slapped himself in the forehead like an exclamation point.

Of course they have security cameras. They are rich.

"Yes," Bob said, "they don't want anyone to steal their Cat Vacs." Bob laughed at his own joke. He was the only one who did. "Anyway, so stay hidden behind the hedge. I'll go ahead and leave the note. Then I'll rejoin you."

"Then what?" Nate whispered.

"Then we wait." He headed away from them.

Sandra put her head down and followed, and the grunt she heard to her right signaled that Nate had gotten underway again as well.

They made good time, and when they hit the mowed clearing, the ground evened out, and they were able to speed up. Within a few minutes, they arrived at the coveted hedge, and Nate collapsed into the meager morning shade it offered. Sandra fought not to roll her eyes as she looked at Bob. "What do we do if someone comes?"

Bob looked back at the woods from whence they'd come. "Run." His face exploded into a lopsided grin she found both endearing and frustrating and then he vanished.

"Where'd he go?" Nate's head swiveled in a panic.

She collapsed onto the ground beside him, and though she hadn't felt particularly warm on their trek, the ground felt blessedly cool. "Get used to it. He likes to disappear on people, got a flair for the dramatic."

"He's really not what I pictured," he whispered.

"Yeah, I gathered that. But don't underestimate him. He'll surprise you."

And then he was there beside her again, sitting in the dirt as if he'd been there all along.

"That was quick," Nate said.

"I told you," she said.

Bob rolled over onto his belly and peered out through a hole between the bottoms of the bushes.

"Can you see anything like that?" she asked.

"Not really." He sounded surprised and disappointed. He pushed himself back up to a seated position and started breaking branches so he could have a small peep hole between the bushes.

"Can't you just hover in the sky and watch?"

She glared at her husband, not appreciating his critical tone, but he was oblivious to her silent scolding.

"Of course I can, but I thought it would be nice to hang out with you guys."

Aww. She was touched. She spun around on her butt and started breaking branches to make her own peep hole.

"Don't shake the bushes too much," Nate scolded, as if he were the expert. "They'll see you!"

"Brendan's not home," Bob said. "It's just Daphne and the girls."

This news unsettled Sandra.

"How do you know that?" Again with the criticism. Was Nate feeling threatened by the angel, and if so, wasn't that a little silly? He was an *angel.*

"I can hear them."

"You can *hear* that he's not there?"

Bob finally sounded annoyed with his critic. "No, but I would be able to *hear* him if he was."

"You could hear him just sitting there doing nothing?"

Sandra tried to sew her husband's lips shut with her mind.

"No, but I would be able to hear him breathing. Right now I can hear your adrenal glands releasing adrenaline."

Nate looked down at his torso as if to verify his adrenal glands were doing this, but he didn't seem to know where those glands were, so he looked at Sandra instead.

"I told you," she said through gritted teeth, "not to underestimate him. Superman hearing is just one of his many abilities."

Bob snorted. "Superman."

"Bob, do you know where Brendan is right now?"

"No idea."

"What if he comes home while we're sitting out here?"

"He won't be able to see us."

She wasn't so sure.

Nate finally succumbed to creating his own peep hole, and then soon they were all sitting perfectly still, peering through the hedge.

"Are you sure the cameras can't see our eyeballs?" Nate asked.

"No," Bob said.

Thirty seconds went by.

"Are you sure she's going to come out of the house, today?" Nate asked.

"No," Bob said.

Ten seconds went by.

"What if she doesn't?" Nate asked.

"Nate!" Sandra said.

"What?"

"Be quiet!"

He was quiet.

They sat there for what felt like forever. Except for the random swat at a mosquito, it was a peaceful wait. The shade began to shrink as the sun rose in the sky and as the temperature rose, the mosquitoes headed for the cooler temperatures of the trees.

The sun on Sandra's back made her sleepy, and just when she was having trouble focusing, she saw, through her tiny field of vision, a little girl come around the edge of the mansion. She opened her mouth to let her partners know that there was a small Barney on the scene when the usually-masculine man beside her let out a shriek that rivaled any terrified cheerleader.

Sandra's first thought was that her husband was terrified of the small Barney, and she couldn't imagine how this could be. She didn't take her eyes off the little girl, who of course, had now turned and was staring directly at them.

There was a scuffle as Bob scooted around her to deal with whatever ridiculous crisis had suddenly befell her husband.

And then the little girl turned and sprinted for the front door, and Sandra turned to glare at her husband.

"What the—"

The sickly pallor of his face dialed her rage back from a ten to a nine. "What happened?" she asked through clenched teeth.

Bob held a small snake up to show her and then tossed it behind them into the lawn.

"Why'd you do that?" Nate asked, breathless. "Now it can just come back."

"We should go," Bob said.

"No!" Sandra didn't want to leave, not after all this work.

"I'm pretty sure our cover's blown," Bob said. "You guys should go."

"No!" Sandra said again. "She just went to get her mother. She'll be here in seconds. If we leave now, she'll be able to see us going across the lawn. We're better off hiding here."

The front door opened, and Daphne and the B—Sandra was pretty sure it was Beatrice—stepped out onto the porch. The sight of Daphne made Sandra's stomach turn. How could she possibly look that perfect so early in the morning, when she hadn't even left the house yet? She wore a pale yellow sleeveless button-up blouse and olive capris, an outfit that made her look like a frail flower. Her perfect blond hair was coiled on top of her head in a poofy bun. Sandra wanted to go find that snake and slip it up her pant leg. But Daphne wasn't completely perfect, because she was obviously disinterested in her daughter's crisis.

The small Barney pointed directly at them and said something Sandra couldn't hear.

"It's okay. It's probably just a bird." Daphne's mind was obviously elsewhere. Then her eyes drifted to her vehicle and she saw the note. *Jackpot.* "Beatrice, go inside."

"But, *Mommy!*"

"Now!" Daphne pushed her inside and shut the door. Then Daphne stared directly at them with such intensity that Sandra was sure she could see them. Sandra held her breath. Slowly, Daphne came down off the porch and headed for her vehicle. As her feet crunched on the gravel, she looked around in every direction. She could probably feel their eyes on her, but she didn't seem to know where that feeling was coming from.

She snatched the note from under her wiper blade and unfolded it. Sandra could feel Bob smiling beside her. Daphne read it in an instant and then her eyes whipped around her property again. Suddenly, Sandra was certain they were about to get caught. Daphne headed straight for them, and Sandra pulled her eyes away from the approaching psychopath to look at Bob for help. But he was no longer there. Argh! That angel!

Sandra started to panic and was getting up to make a run for it. She knew she could outrun Daphne Barney. She wasn't sure her husband could, though. Then she heard an approaching engine and she froze. This had just gotten so much worse. Brendan Barney was home. She looked at Nate. "Run!" she hissed and turned to go, but then from behind the house there was an explosion of shattering glass. The angel! She didn't know if Bob had actually broken something or had just made the noise for a diversion, but it worked. Daphne turned and headed that way as her husband parked his truck.

"What's wrong?" Brendan called out.

Sandra couldn't see him, but the sound of his voice gave her the shivers.

"I just heard breaking glass in the backyard." Daphne sounded so terrified that Sandra actually felt guilty.

"Glass? There isn't any glass in the backyard."

"Yes, I know. Will you go check it out?"

"What's that?" Brendan asked.

Daphne shoved their bluff note into the pocket of her wrinkle-free capris. "Nothing."

Brendan stepped closer to her and into Sandra's sight. "Tell me what it is."

Daphne turned away from him. "I just wrote a to-do list to remind myself of everything I have to do today. Now, will you please go see if someone's in the backyard?"

Brendan headed that way, and after one more glance in Sandra's direction, Daphne followed her husband. As soon as they rounded the corner of the building and went out of sight, Sandra turned to her husband and said, "Run!" again. And this time, they ran.

Chapter 34

"Did you really break something?" Sandra asked. She was out of breath, leaning against the chicken barn with her hands on her knees.

"Nah." Bob sounded smug. "It was just a sound effect."

He never ceased to amaze. "It was a very convincing one," she said between ragged breaths.

"I think I'm having a heart attack." Nate clutched his chest, but she could tell by looking at him that he was going to be just fine.

She struggled to stand up straight. "Okay, now what?"

Bob made a weird clicking sound with his tongue. "I'm not sure there is a next. I'm wondering if that entire mission was a waste." He looked at her. "We didn't learn much."

"Yes, we did!" she cried. "We learned that *she's* probably the killer."

Nate stood up straight too. "What makes you say that?"

"She didn't show the note to her husband."

"So?" Nate said. "That just means that *he's* the killer, and she is scared of him and what he might do if he saw the note."

"See?" Bob interjected. "We didn't learn anything."

Sandra looked at her minivan, longing for its air conditioning. "Well, aside from sneaking into her house, is there another way to spy on her?"

Bob looked contemplative, as if he were mentally scanning a list of possibilities. "No."

Well, *that* was definitive. And she wasn't sure she even believed him. Maybe there just wasn't an *ethical* way to continue spying on her.

"Why don't you two take a break from the spying," Bob said, and Sandra couldn't help inferring that he was also suggesting they were terrible at it. "And I'll go back and watch the yard again. I'm not going into the house, but I'll just keep an eye on the general property."

Sandra agreed to the plan. "No middle school sports commitments today?"

Panic flickered across his face. "Yes. This afternoon I have cheering camp."

Sandra snorted. "Cheering camp?"

Bob bristled. "Yes, cheering camp. Cheerleading is a sport, you know."

Sandra wasn't sure what to say. She'd never really thought about it. "Okay, we'll go home. I need a shower." She headed for the minivan, hardly caring whether her husband followed her.

Only when she placed her hands on the steering wheel did she realize the oddity of what she'd just done. Why was she in the driver's seat? When the two of them went somewhere, Nate *always* drove. Yet, right now, she hadn't even thought about it. She's just wearily climbed in. She watched him open the passenger side door and climb in beside her, waiting for him to remark on the role reversal.

But he didn't. He just reclined the seat with a thump. He threw an arm over his eyes and said, "Honestly, I don't know how you do this."

She snickered and turned the key in the ignition. "Do what?"

"Fight crime." He moved his arm away from his face and turned toward her. "I mean, you willingly put yourself into these situations. I thought I'd been missing out, and I guess that's true, but I didn't realize how *not fun* your little adventures are."

She wasn't sure if she was being scolded or praised. "As much as I love spending time with you, honey, you don't have to join me for these adventures."

"You're right. I think it's important for couples to have individual hobbies. I really hate snakes."

She laughed. "Me too."

"Maybe. But you didn't scream like a little girl."

She bit back a snicker. "You did just fine."

"Even so, I'm resigning. As long as you're with the angel, I'm going to stay out of it." He shifted in his seat. "I mean, I'd rather you resign too, but I doubt that's going to happen. But either way, I now know that this is not my calling."

"That's okay, honey. This was a weird morning. We don't usually hide behind a hedge for hours waiting for garter snakes to attack."

"What a relief. I'm going to take a nap now."

___

SANDRA WAS ALMOST HOME when her phone rang. She swiped the green icon. "Hello?"

At first, there was no response, and Sandra thought it was Tiara again.

It wasn't. "Hello." The voice sounded familiar and some part of Sandra's stomach recognized it well enough to be unsettled by it. But it took several seconds for Sandra's brain to catch up. "You could have just rung the doorbell, you know."

Yikes. "I'm sorry," Sandra tried, "I don't know what you—"

"Save it. I know it was you. What I can't figure out is what you did in the backyard. I can't find any broken glass anywhere, and I know you didn't have time to pick it up."

Sandra thought silence was her best bet.

Nate rolled his head toward her and opened one eye.

For a second, she steered with her knee so she could hold a finger up to her lips to shush him.

He opened his other eye and sat up.

"What do you want?" Daphne asked.

She didn't know how to answer that.

Daphne didn't give her much time to think about it. "Name your price. I'll meet it. A bag of cash for the videos, and then we're done. If you come at me again, I won't be so cooperative. I figure it'll cost me about the same to pay you off or to have you taken care of. Don't make me regret my choice."

Oh my word, this woman is as cold as ice. She had no idea what to say.

"So?" She was growing impatient. "What's your price?"

Sandra panicked. "A hundred thousand dollars."

Nate's eyes widened.

Daphne sighed into the phone. "Fine. Do you have a pen? I'll give you the address."

"Yes, hang on a sec." Sandra tried to calmly steer the van onto the shoulder, but it was more like a sudden yank to the right that sent them both hurdling left. The driver behind her laid on his horn as he sped past her with fury on his face.

"You made that guy mad."

"Who was that?" Daphne snapped. "Who's with you?"

"No one," Sandra quickly lied. "It's the radio. Okay, I've got a pen." This too was a lie. She reached into the glove box and started rooting around for one. She pulled out seventy-five Five Guys napkins, at least as many bank deposit slips, some chopsticks, two packets of mayonnaise, a pacifier, and a pair of pantyhose that she fervently hoped were hers—but no pen. This couldn't be happening.

Daphne was already giving the address.

"Hang on, I need paper."

Daphne growled into the phone.

She grabbed a deposit slip and a lipstick from her purse. "Okay, go ahead."

"Old Black Farm Road," Daphne said with painful slowness. "In Chesterville. There's a barn. I'll be in it with your money. Bring the videos in with you. No funny business."

Chesterville? Why Chesterville? But she didn't argue. "Okay, when?"

"Eleven o'clock tonight. If you're late, the deal's off." The phone went silent.

Sandra sat there staring at the phone in her hand, wondering what had just happened.

"You need to talk to Bob."

She nodded. "I sure do."

"I'm not letting you go to Chesterville without him."

"I know that. And don't worry, I wouldn't." Chesterville was a tiny town north of Plainfield. It wasn't on the way to anywhere. If Daphne planned to lure her out into the woods to kill her, Chesterville would be a logical choice. Sandra hadn't ever met someone who actually lived in Chesterville, and she couldn't think of a single business that made its home there. If she remembered correctly, even the post office had gone out of business. The place was a ghost town.

"Maybe you should even tell the police too. They could follow you there, back you up."

"Maybe." She didn't think that was a good idea, though. Chip and Slaughter would take over and not allow her anywhere near Chesterville. Besides, she was confident that she didn't need them, not when she had Bob. She would catch Daphne and tie her up in a neat bow for the professionals, just like Bob and she had done last time.

Piece of cake.

Chapter 35

Sandra had kissed the kids good night and tucked them in, and now sat in the kitchen staring at her front door—though of course, if Bob arrived, he probably wouldn't use the door.

The clocks in her house all disagreed as to exactly what time it was, but they were all within spitting distance of nine o'clock, and yet she still hadn't heard from her angel friend. She was starting to panic, but her husband was already well past panicville.

"You need to call the cops, Sandra! I don't want to go with you, and I'm not going to let you go alone! Why on earth hasn't Bob given you a way to get in touch with him?"

"Because he's an angel," she said for the thousandth time. What *was* she going to do if Bob didn't show in time? She didn't know, but Nate's harping on it wasn't helping her to decide. She put her head in her hands. "Please, stop! You're driving me crazy."

His mouth snapped shut. "I'm sorry. I just love you so much, and I'm not going to let anything happen to you."

She took a deep breath. "I know this. But what I'm saying—the part you're not yet hearing—is that *I* won't put myself in danger. I promise."

He plunked down into a kitchen chair. "You got yourself shoved into a trunk."

How long was he going to hold that over her head? "That wasn't my fault! I didn't willingly climb into the trunk!"

They then engaged in a staring contest, and though it was a tense moment, Sandra was grateful that it was also a quiet one.

Bob broke the silence. "Why the long faces?"

"There you are!" Nate cried.

Bob drew his brows together. "What's wrong?"

"Nothing's wrong. What have you seen?" Sandra needed the facts. Fast.

"I've been hanging out in the Barney driveway, as promised. But I think they went to bed. All the lights are off."

I doubt they're both *in bed.* "Okay, Bob, listen up. There's not much time." She filled him in as efficiently as she could, trying not to be annoyed by Nate's umpteen unhelpful interruptions.

When she finished, Bob's jaw hung open.

"What? You don't think this is a good idea?"

"Of course I don't think it's a good idea! You're going to take a payoff!"

She barked out a laugh. "Of course not!" Was he an imbecile? "I'm just going to make her *think* I'm going to take the money. In the meantime, I'll get her to confess, and then we'll tie her up or something and call the police."

"*We'll* tie her up? You mean you want me to let her see me?"

Sandra rapidly shook her head. Had she done *that* bad of a job sharing her plan? "No, I just need you to thump her on the head or something and then I'll tie her up."

"I hate this plan," Nate said.

They both ignored him.

"Okay, let's go," Bob said. "Did you already pack the rope?"

She grabbed her purse. "No, but one of Joanna's jump ropes is tangled around one of the backseats of the van."

Bob raised an eyebrow. "You sure that'll be sturdy enough?"

Sandra kissed her husband on the cheek. "We're tying up a Stepford wife, not the Hulk. It'll be fine." She looked at Nate. "I love you. I'll text you when it's over, and then I'll come right home. Don't worry."

"Yeah, right. Anyway that I can stop this?"

She stopped and looked at him. "Sure. If you tell me not to go, I won't go." *Please don't say that, please don't say that.*

He nodded. "I'm not going to test that promise." He looked at Bob. "You'll take care of her?"

"Of course."

"Okay then." He looked at her. "I love you too."

Before he could change his mind, she hurried out the door.

Bob teleported into the front passenger seat and waited for her to buckle up before saying, "He's a good man, your husband."

"I know." She started the car and when she looked over her shoulder to back up, she realized Bob was giving her a skeptical look. "I really do know. Today has just been ... a lot." She tried to think of a tactful way to express what she was feeling. She wasn't angry with Nate, exactly, so what was it? "We just have ... different investigative styles."

Bob laughed. "Yes, I think that is true."

The closer she got to Chesterville, the harder her hitchhiking butterflies worked to commandeer her stomach. "So, I'm going to walk into the barn and just get her talking, right?"

"That's what you said the plan was."

"Do you have a better plan?" She wished he did.

"Not really. This one worked with the last guy. Might as well try it again."

She thought this particular murderer was a bit more dangerous than the last. "All right then."

"I sense hesitation. You don't have to go through with this. We can call the police right now, and let them take it from here. It would be pretty suspicious to find Daphne in a barn in Chesterville with a hundred thousand dollars in cash."

Sandra couldn't bear the thought of letting them have all the fun. "Nope, I'm all in."

"Glad to hear it. Your turn is just up ahead."

Her headlights lit up a small green sign that read Old Black Farm Road. The road's name had sounded so innocent when Daphne had spoken it, but now seeing the words in print made them seem far more ominous. Or maybe it was just the thick darkness of the night; the clouds prevented them from enjoying the company of the stars or moon. Or maybe it was the isolation of the meeting. Old Black Farm Road stretched out in front of her like a long, narrow black ribbon. It went on and on, and the deeper into the forest she drove, the narrower the road got until leaves scraped both sides of her van as she crawled along into the unknown.

Just when she was about to give up and try to turn around, Bob pointed toward a giant dark rectangle looming to their left. She slowed the van, unsure of what she was looking at. Was that really a barn? Who would build a barn way out here? She stopped the car. Someone a very long time ago, that's who. The ancient barn stood across the narrow lane from an equally ancient farmhouse. Both buildings were dark and still. She pulled the van in front of the barn and as her headlights lit up the eerie building, she took a long look before turning off the van. It was old, for sure, but it still looked sturdy. This was encouraging. She took the keys out of the ignition so that her automatic headlights would turn off faster, and then she looked at Bob in the darkness.

Without the engine running, the silence was almost overwhelming. She sensed he was going to say something and cut him off, "Don't even ask," she whispered. "Yes, I'm doing this. It's Daphne Barney for crying out loud. How dangerous can this really be?" She opened her door and the interior light seemed unreasonably bright. She got out as quickly and quietly as possible and then softly clicked the door shut behind her, staying rooted to her spot until the light faded out and returned them to darkness. It may only be Daphne Barney, but her heart was still trying to thump its way out of her chest.

What was that awful smell? She concentrated on it for a moment in order to identify it. And once she recognized it, she wondered what had taken her so long: it was gasoline. Why did this abandoned property smell like gasoline? She opened her mouth to ask if Bob could smell it, but then she snapped her mouth shut. First of all, don't talk to the invisible angel in front of the murderer, and second, of course he could smell it. Bob had a super sniffer.

She slid her phone out of her back pocket and turned on the flashlight. Then she followed the beam of light toward the barn, whose giant front door stood open a few feet, just wide enough for her to walk through.

She stepped into the barn, and the temperature dropped twenty degrees. She shined her light around the tall walls, and the space looked giant—and empty. Where was Daphne? Even before visually confirming that the barn was empty, she had sensed that there was no one else there. In fact, she sensed that there had been no one else there for a very long time. Just as she was thinking about turning around, there was a small scuttling noise at the back end of the barn. It didn't sound like a noise a person would make. A small animal, probably. Surely mice and other little critters had made their home in this cavernous building by now. She wanted to ask Bob what he wanted to do, but she didn't want to speak to him. He walked deeper into the barn, and so she followed, even though she didn't see the point.

The gasoline smell grew stronger, and with it, her unease. She really wanted to go, but she still didn't dare speak this desire aloud, so she simply turned toward the door and hoped that Bob would figure out her intent. As she turned, a loud grating sound rang out as the old barn door slid shut in front of her. Without thinking, she ran toward it, but she reached it long after it had closed. She grabbed the door and tried to push it open again, and the rattling of chains outside made her blood run cold. She whirled around to look at Bob, but he was right beside her. She stared at him wide-eyed as if to say, "Help me push on the door!"

But he held up one finger: *Wait.*

Wait for what? They were locked in a creepy barn in Chesterville! She stared at him, trying to figure out what they were waiting for, and then she heard a crackling noise. She didn't recognize the sound at first, but then she smelled smoke.

Chapter 36

With an authority that gave Sandra chills, Bob swung his arm out to his side and the barn door flew open with a crash. It moved so fast that Sandra heard the chains hit the ground after the fact. A horse whinnied somewhere nearby, and for a second, Sandra panicked that the horse was in the barn. Bob took her hand and led her outside, as if she needed encouragement to get out of a burning barn. Sandra looked back to see that Daphne had placed hay along the front wall of the barn—hay that had probably been christened with gasoline. Flames slowly licked the barn walls, but she knew they would soon pick up in power and do more than lick.

"Do you have a signal?" Bob was all business.

She looked down at her phone.

A blur raced pass them with such speed that Sandra might not have known what it was if not for the galloping hoofbeats giving it away. Sandra looked up to see the back of a horse headed farther up Old Black Farm Road. Where did she think she was going? "She was going to burn us alive and then ride off like it never happened?" Sandra had underestimated this woman's evil.

"Not *us. You.*" He threw her a glance. "Do you have a signal?" he asked again, sounding impatient.

She looked down. "I have one bar."

"Good. Call the fire department. I will stop her."

She was alone with her phone. She dialed 911 and gave them as much information as she could think to give, including the name of the arsonist she had just watched ride away on horseback. The operator sounded incredulous, but Sandra repeated the information and then hung up. She didn't want to stand there beside a burning barn talking on the phone. She jumped into her minivan, backed away from the burning building, and followed after the horse. She was certain that she had never been so furious in her life. She could not wait to see Daphne Barney in handcuffs and an orange jumpsuit. She suspected it was tough to keep those outfits wrinkle-free.

The road narrowed to nothing but a path, and Sandra started to fear that her van soon wouldn't fit between the trees—but she persisted. The path appeared to abruptly end in front of her, and she slowed to a crawl. Then she saw that the road curved away from her, and she slowly stuck the nose of her minivan around the corner.

She exhaled in relief. The horse stood immediately in front of her, in the middle of the road, with Daphne perched on its back. She left her headlights on, but she turned off the engine and locked the doors. If Daphne was going to steal the minivan for a quick getaway, she would have to fight Sandra for the keys first.

Daphne did not even acknowledge her existence, so Sandra slowly walked up alongside the horse. Daphne looked down at her, her face as white as a ghost. Sandra didn't know what to say. Why was Daphne the terrified one? Sandra decided on, "What are you doing?" This was a pretty pathetic getaway.

"There's something in the path." Daphne's voice wavered.

Sandra looked ahead of the horse. "I don't see anything." She tried to keep the smirk out of her voice.

"I know, but the horse won't move past it. He's scared of something. There's something there." The horse whinnied as if in agreement.

"So, turn around and go the other way." This didn't make much sense, as Sandra's minivan was now blocking the path.

"I tried that. The horse won't move." The woman was genuinely terrified. Served her right. She looked down at her again and started, as if just noticing she was there, or just realizing who she was. "How did you get out of the barn?"

Not going to answer that. "So, you're just going to sit there on your horse after you tried to burn me alive?"

It was her turn not to answer.

"I've called the cops. They're on their way, along with the fire department."

This spurred Daphne into action, and she yanked her reins to the left, but her horse reared up and then came crashing back down, efficiently refusing to move, no matter how hard Daphne drove her heels into his sides.

Sandra stumbled backward to get out of the way and almost went down on her rump.

"What's happening?" Daphne cried. "There's something here!" In a panic, she jerked the reins to the right, but the horse just spun in a circle.

Sandra wondered if Bob had learned this trick from the angel who'd stopped Balaam's donkey on the road to Balak. She wished Bob would make the horse talk to Daphne. She would've loved to hear what he had to say. This idea made Sandra laugh out loud.

Daphne looked down at her in horror. "What's so funny?"

Sandra felt guilty. Nothing was funny. A man had been murdered. "Why did you kill Phoenix?"

"I don't have to say anything to you," Daphne spat.

Sandra folded her arms across her chest. "Fine. We can just sit here quietly, in this exact spot, waiting for the bright lights and sirens."

"I'll give you all the money I have," Daphne hissed. "Just get me out of here." She glanced at the locked up minivan.

"Maybe. Tell me why you killed Phoenix."

"Oh, what does it matter?" Daphne wailed in frustration.

"It matters to Phoenix's loved ones."

"That man didn't have any loved ones!"

"You're wrong."

"Whatever. If he had just stayed out of our lives and minded his own business, he'd be still be alive."

They heard the faint whine of distant sirens, and Daphne tried to get her horse going again, but it just whinnied and spun in place.

"So you killed a man just because he was related to your family?"

"I don't care who is *related* to anybody. This is about money." She glanced at the minivan again. "Something you could have plenty of if you would stop being such a fool. Think of your children. Think about what money could do for them. Private schools. College—"

"You killed Phoenix because he was going to steal part of your inheritance?"

"Not *part* of it. *All* of it!"

What? That didn't make any sense. How was he going to do that? Something clicked in Sandra's brain. She gasped. "Brendan isn't Richard's biological son?" No wonder he was so short!

She didn't answer, but her silence was answer enough.

Sandra still didn't understand. "Surely Richard would've split the inheritance, if he even included Phoenix at all."

"Richard *hates* Brendan," she hissed.

The sirens grew louder. Soon, Sandra wouldn't be able to ask any more questions. "So you honestly think Richard would have left his money to a *stranger*, rather than the son he's known his whole life?"

She glared down from her perch. "You don't know these people. Richard would have been so thrilled to be able to do just that. He would have done it just to spite Brendan. Phoenix would have been the son Richard never had. And my girls would have been left with nothing." The sirens were closing in.

"So you framed your father-in-law? That's pretty diabolical."

"That wasn't the plan." She looked around frantically, a rabbit caught in a trap.

"How did you even have that bat?"

She groaned. "Because none of those hillbillies pick up after themselves, and somehow that bat got left behind, so my stupid father-in-law picked it up and threw it in our vehicle. Look, I didn't go there to kill that guy. I met him at the church to pay him off, but he wouldn't listen to me ..." She started to cry. "He was crazy, just like you, said he didn't care about money. If he'd just taken it, he wouldn't be dead right now."

The sirens grew louder. Sandra knew she only had seconds. "But why did you kill him?"

"I just got so angry. He wouldn't listen. When he turned to walk away from me, I just ... I just ... I followed him into the woods. I was just so *mad*. I just wanted to get rid of him." Her voice dropped an octave on the last four words, and Sandra's arms broke out in goosebumps.

She didn't believe her that it wasn't planned. "You're full of it. You were obviously wearing gloves, because they didn't find your prints on the bat." She was wearing gloves now, so this was a fair assumption. "And you snuck the bat *back* into the bat bag, with Richard's prints and Phoenix's blood still on it. Don't tell me this all just *happened*."

Daphne kicked the horse again.

Sandra felt horrible for the animal, but wasn't sure how to rescue him. She didn't think she could wrestle Daphne off a horse. *I should try to distract her, keep her talking.* What else could she ask? What did she need to know? "How long had you known Phoenix?"

"A few days. He came to the house once. I told him if I ever saw him again that I'd make sure he went to prison." She laughed shrilly. "I told him I can get creative with my lies, and not to test me."

"But he did test you, didn't he? He came to the church softball game? And you called the cops?"

"Fat lot of good that did. Took them two hours to show up."

This wasn't difficult to believe. "And you just happened to have a burner phone in your purse?" Sandra was proud of herself for calling it a burner phone.

"You'd have a burner too if your husband was always snooping through your phone, reading your messages, seeing what websites you visit ..."

Good grief, this was one wacko family. "So Phoenix ran from the police, not because he was guilty of anything, but because you'd threatened to have him thrown into prison?"

"How should I know why he ran? Get out of the road!" she screamed into the darkness.

Sandra imagined that Bob was enjoying this. "And now you're the one going to prison. Why'd you take his wallet?"

"Didn't want anyone to know who he was." Daphne looked down at her with disdain. "Are you really going to turn down all this money and let them catch me?"

"There's nowhere to go, Daphne. I can't go back the way I came. The police are obviously on this road now, blocking our path. And even if I could get around your horse, the road is too narrow."

"No!" she cried, as if she suddenly had hope of escape. "The road widens out just ahead and attaches to another real road, which my friend lives on. This is her horse!"

"You have a friend?"

Half of Daphne's red lips curled up in a sneer. "Money can buy you lots of things. Let me show you."

"Daphne, I wouldn't take your money if it was the last money on earth."

The blue lights came into view and the sirens stopped.

"Did you even ever have the videos?"

Sandra could feel her fury from where she stood. "How could I? Didn't you delete them from the church computer?"

"Yes, but I thought you'd figured out a way to get them back. I'm no computer whiz."

They heard men's voices and car doors slamming behind the minivan, and Sandra smiled at Bob, even though she couldn't see him.

Daphne looked down at her and asked, with a voice like ice, "You know what's in the road, don't you?"

Chapter 37

The blue lights were blinding, and Sandra could feel a headache starting. At least they'd turned the sirens off. She was grateful for that. She imagined the horse was too. It didn't need to be further traumatized.

Sandra had been worried about the horse. It had been stolen and then confronted by an angel, but Slaughter seemed to speak horse, and was doing a great job of comforting the beautiful beast. She'd already made a call to someone who was coming to rescue the animal, make sure he was okay, and then bring him home. Sandra wished someone would do the same for her.

As Sandra had anticipated, it was wonderfully comforting to see Daphne in handcuffs. Sandra quietly watched as Chip pulled her off the horse, slapped the cuffs on her, and then led her toward a waiting police car.

At first, Chip ignored Sandra entirely, and only Dwight, her least favorite soccer ref, stopped to ask her questions. She answered them as vaguely as she could and counted the seconds until she could get out of there. But then Chip fit her into his schedule. "I guess I shouldn't be surprised!" he called out as he headed her way.

She didn't respond. What was there to say?

"You want to tell me why Daphne Barney tried to burn down a barn with you in it?"

Sandra shrugged. "I guess she knew that I was onto her."

"And you just followed her out here all by yourself in the middle of nowhere to meet up with her in an abandoned barn?"

Sandra bit the inside of her cheek to keep from smiling. Chip didn't appear to be in the smiling mood. "Yes."

He raised an eyebrow. "Yes? That's all you're going to say?"

"What do you want me to say, Chip?"

"I want you to tell me how you knew she was the killer."

"I didn't know, exactly. I just knew it was one of them, and she's the one who tried to burn down an old barn with me in it."

"There are chains on the ground near the barn door. She didn't try to trap you inside?"

Sandra didn't know how to answer that. "I'm not sure what her plan was."

"What I'm asking is, how did you get out of the barn?"

"I just walked out."

He raised his voice, and several other police officers turned to stare at them. "She lured you into a barn and lit it on fire, but she didn't think to shut the door and lock you inside?"

Sandra shrugged. "I'm not sure. You'll need to ask her. I don't think she's a very talented criminal."

Chip stepped closer to her and lowered his voice. "The thing is, Sandra. I did ask her. She claims that she chained the barn door shut, and that you magically were able to escape. So, I want an explanation."

She'd never been so tongue-tied. Why couldn't Bob rescue her now?

"You're not going to say anything?"

Her head was throbbing. "I'm sorry, Chip." She sounded like a mouse. "I just don't have any answers for you."

He looked at the horse. "And then she tried to get away on horseback and you chased her down a skidder trail in a minivan? You can see how hard all this is for me to believe, right?"

"It's got really good tires."

Chip laughed, but he still managed to look angry. "Sandra, I am not a stupid man. I know there's more you're not telling me. You're lucky I believe that you are one of the good guys. Otherwise, I'd be mighty suspicious of you. Last fall, someone tries to shoot you and just mysteriously has an arm seizure. Last winter, someone falls through the ice and you and your kid are mysteriously able to pull him out. And now, you are mysteriously able to escape from a burning barn with the door chained shut and then you mysteriously paralyzed a horse. I don't believe in the paranormal, Sandra. So I need you to explain to me what's happening here."

Sandra was suddenly beyond uncomfortable. This was no longer funny. Chip knew too much. She wished she could become invisible and fly away like Bob. She tried to look respectful and servile. "I'm sorry, I'm not trying to be difficult. But I've been through a lot, and I'm really not feeling well. Do you think I could go home now?"

He stared at her long and hard before granting her permission. "We're not done talking about this yet."

She glanced back at her beloved minivan with the spectacular tires. "It seems I'm blocked in by about fourteen vehicles. Do you think one of your officers could give me a ride?"

He nodded, his jaw tight, and motioned Dwight over.

Sandra groaned. She'd rather walk home than hitch a ride with Dwight, but it was too late to specify which chauffeur she preferred, and she didn't want to do anything to further perplex Chip. So, she would take a ride home from her least favorite soccer ref, and she would be grateful. It could be worse.

Chapter 38

Friday night brought a rematch at Grace Evangelical. But New Hope showed up with a very different team than they'd had the last time the two teams had gone head to head. Though Richard had been released from police custody with no charges, he had apparently lost his taste for softball. No one was surprised that Brendan Barney didn't show up either.

Nate, Pastor, Boomer, and Loriana were there, along with five Bickfords. No one mentioned the ridiculous new "rules" forbidding the Bickfords from playing. Maybe Pastor had realized they'd never been a good idea.

For reasons Sandra didn't understand, this time when Peter asked to play, he was told yes and sent to right field. He was elated. Ton Truck, apparently encouraged by Peter's success, asked again to pitch and was promptly shut down.

Grace E's pitcher was *fast*, but that didn't bother the Bickfords. New Hope's leadoff batter easily reached first, as did his brother after that and their cousin after that. When Pastor Cliff stepped up to bat fourth, a cleanup position that could only have been assigned by the Pastor himself, there was a Bickford on every bag.

Pastor swung at the first pitch and missed. The pitcher threw a change-up, and Pastor swung and missed again. Now he looked nervous. He didn't usually strike out, he wasn't *that* bad, but they didn't usually face such tricky pitching. He swung at the third pitch and just barely got a piece of it. It fell nearly right in front of him, and the catcher immediately scooped it up and tagged home plate. Sandra looked down at the book to record that out, so she didn't see the rest of the play, but she *heard* it. Apparently, the catcher then wound the ball to the second baseman who then wound it to first for the first triple play Sandra had ever seen. Well, technically, she hadn't *seen* this one either, but she was never going to admit that.

Grace E whooped and bounced their way off the field as Pastor trudged toward the dugout with his head down. When he came within three feet of Ton Truck, he glanced up and said, "You go ahead and pitch an inning."

This cheered the Bickfords up a bit, and Ton Truck struck out Grace E's first three batters, effectively taking the wind out of their sails. Sandra knew then that Grace E didn't have a prayer. If their first three batters couldn't hit off Ton Truck, none of them would be able to. Ton Truck collapsed onto the old wooden bench beside her, making the whole thing wobble beneath them.

"That's some good pitching!"

"Thank ya." He spit into the dirt, and she tried not to visibly cringe. "So, I hear you're the one who caught that murderer."

"Sort of."

He winked at her. "Pretty impressive."

"Thank ya."

Nate joined them then, sitting on the other side of her and reaching out to tickle his youngest under the chin.

"That little guy's gonna know a lot about ball, just sitting there watchin' every game," Ton Truck said. He cleared his throat loudly.

Sandra had her doubts that Sammy was actually *watching*, but she didn't argue. It was soon Ton Truck's turn to bat, and he left her husband and her alone in the dugout.

"Kind of weird here without any Barneys," he said.

"Yes, but pleasant too."

"I never minded Richard, but you're right that Brendan was a little unpleasant."

"And now we know why. He was living with a murderer." Her phone vibrated, and she glanced down at it.

"Is it Detective Chip again?"

"No. It says spam." She declined the call. "Chip stopped calling after that first day."

"Really? I'm surprised. You never answered any of his questions, did you?"

"No, I sure didn't, but ..." She stopped talking long enough to get the scorebook caught up. "He told me he didn't believe in the paranormal," she said under her breath. "I think that, when he really thought about it, he figured out that if I ever did answer his questions, he might not like the answers I'd give."

"Mm-hmm," Nate said contemplatively. "That makes sense. He might have decided it would be easier to just stay in the dark."

"You're on deck."

"I know." He leaned over and kissed her on the cheek. "Even so, maybe you should lie low next time crime comes to town. Maybe your supernatural assistant doesn't *want* to be found out."

She knew he didn't, especially since she hadn't seen hide nor hair of him since he'd left her standing beside the burning barn. "Maybe," she mused. Then she kissed her husband back. "But I'm not making any promises."

BOOKS BY ROBIN MERRILL

Wing and a Prayer Mysteries
The Whistle Blower
The Showstopper
The Pinch Runner

Gertrude, Gumshoe Cozy Mystery Series
Introducing Gertrude, Gumshoe
Gertrude, Gumshoe: Murder at Goodwill
Gertrude, Gumshoe and the VardSale Villain
Gertrude, Gumshoe: Slam Is Murder
Gertrude, Gumshoe: Gunslinger City
Gertrude, Gumshoe and the Clearwater Curse

Shelter Trilogy
Shelter
Daniel
Revival

Piercehaven Trilogy
Piercehaven
Windmills
Trespass

Standalone Stories
Commack
Grace Space: A Direct Sales Tale

Robin also writes sweet romance as Penelope Spark.

Want the inside scoop?
Visit robinmerrill.com to join
Robin's Readers!

Made in the USA
Monee, IL
08 July 2020